NO GRAVESTONE LEFT UNTURNED

GENA SHOWALTER
JILL MONROE

AUTHOR TALK MEDIA

Cover Created by Leni Kauffman

Editing by AZ Editing

Proofreading by Naomi Lane

Chapter Header by AlexZel through CreativeFabrica.com

PROLOGUE

*A*s the flesh melted off her bones, Jane Ladling didn't allow herself to whimper...more than a dozen times. Like everyone else born and raised in Aurelian Hills, Georgia, she knew how to thrive amid each of the twelve seasons. Yes, twelve. The town had just escaped the Pollenating and Definitely Probably Spring to enter Summer's First Kiss, a time when cool mornings mutated into sizzling afternoons. Unfortunately, today's sizzling afternoon came with intermittent, tornado-level gusts of wind.

After collecting and disposing of a piece of trash, she blew her bangs out of her eyes. Or tried to. Sweat soaked her brow, making dark hanks of hair adhere to her skin. Didn't help that she wore a thousand pounds of dirt and protective clothing for gardening. Long-sleeved shirt. Overalls. Apron. Gloves. Rubber boots. A backpack of supplies. And a sunhat.

Every day, Jane worked tirelessly to ensure every plot, stone and blade of grass looked its best. As the sole owner and operator of the landlocked Garden of Memories Cemetery, she carried the full weight of responsibility for its maintenance. A thankless job, considering most of the residents had been dead for decades or centuries, but she relished every second. Well, maybe not *every* second.

With only a meager budget supplied by the cemetery's trust, she had to choose between food and proper equipment. Food won, ensuring weed-whacking Wednesday got completed with a pair of shears, a tiny shovel, and a positive attitude.

Massaging her aching lower back, she headed to the final area in need of attention. A spot at the farthest edge of the property known as the Valley of Dolls. She frowned when a flash of white caught the afternoon sun. Was that...?

Oh, no, no, no. She stalked across the distance at a faster clip, closing in on a thick-stemmed, three-foot plant. A gasp caught in her throat. It *was*—and there wasn't just one stalk but many, some already heavy with spiked yellow pods. Why, the area fairly teemed with the stuff.

Her heart sank. Thorn apple. Aka a gardener's worst nightmare, according to her Grandma Lily, God rest her soul. Others sometimes referred to this horror of nature as jimsonweed, the devil's snare, and moonflower. But whatever the name, it was a triple threat: invasive, poisonous, and as rank as stinky feet.

Why hadn't she noticed this infestation yesterday? Or the day before? She'd been fully attentive during her morning rounds. Mostly attentive. Okay, so she'd been a wee bit distracted lately. Not her fault. There was kinda sorta a new man in her life, and he tended to consume her thoughts.

An image of Special Agent Conrad Ryan flashed through her mind. Tall and broad shouldered, with well-defined strength in every part of his body. Thick black hair. Dreamy amber eyes. The best part, all that masculine goodness came with a big, hard, imposing...badge. But she wasn't going to think about him right now. Nope. She had some damage control to do. Exactly how long had the creeping vine grown without her notice?

Nose wrinkling, she withdrew a cell from a pocket of her apron to study this week's security feed of the area. Wait. None of the cameras reached this far out. Dang it!

Grandma Lily's voice suddenly filled her head. *If ever you see this garbage shrub, you gear up and go to war without delay, young lady. You hear me? Thorn apple is a curse. A plague! A disaster in the making.*

Before the dear woman died of cancer a few years back, she'd created a journal filled with notes Jane had photographed and now carried in her phone. She keyed up the one dedicated to thorn apple, written after the eradication of an infestation, and read over the highlighted passages.

Invasive. Highly aggressive. Must be uprooted ASAP or it will overtake the entire 75-acre property. Toxic to animals and people. If seeds are consumed, expect a racing heartbeat, incontinence, hallucinations, and unwarranted hostility. If you survive, that is.

The "toxic to animals" part cinched the deal. There wasn't a more dedicated fur-mom than Jane, who had the honor and privilege of raising Rolex, the world's sweetest cat. The precious darling usually perched at her side while she gardened; thanks to the high velocity of the wind, she'd left him tucked safely inside their cottage.

So. There was no better time to gather and torch this 4x4 patch of thorn apple, sending it back to its maker down below.

Already geared up, Jane grabbed a thick, black trash bag from her backpack. Since this was to be her last weed whacking battle of the day—and the most important—she decided to part with her dwindling supply of water.

She used her canteen to drench the soil, then settled on her knees, wrapped gloved hands around a thick purple stem, and tugged. To her surprise, the roots hadn't yet gripped; they slid free with great ease. Onto the next.

While she worked, wind whistling and sun glaring, she wished at least one person had been buried out here, so she'd have someone to converse with. But this far from the actual grounds, two ancient oaks and their root systems prevented it. Well, prevented it for the once-living.

As a little girl, she'd laid to rest three of her favorite dolls out here. Miss EmmyLou, who'd developed advanced, incurable Cooties. Lady Agnes, who'd caught the dreaded Cattywampus fever. And Prince Snugglebug, who'd "accidentally" fallen out of a tree. Jane had always entertained suspicions about the incident. Pops, Grandma Lily, and Lily's best friend Fiona Lawrence had attended the funerals, wiping pretend tears from their eyes as Jane led the services. Afterwards, the four of them planted wildflowers atop each mound. The buttercups, verbena and thimbleberry now grew in abandon, the blooms a wonderful reminder of favorite childhood memories.

Another sweltering wind kicked up, snatching the sunhat from Jane's head. The wide-brimmed beauty tumbled over bushes before her mind gave the command to give chase. Which she did. Though she flailed and leaped, a new gust carried the hat over a wrought-iron fence and out of sight.

Argh! Earlier, she'd lost her sunglasses. What would be next? Her good sense? Her dignity? Or had she already parted with those?

Sighing, she returned to the thorn apple. Only two stalks to go. After carefully maneuvering one into the trash bag, she turned to the final abomination. The wind blustered again, and the stem bent, slapping her in the mouth. She gasped as a small pellet-like object shot across her tongue. In reflex, she swallowed.

Please be a bug. Please, please, please. But what if she'd ingested thorn apple?

Jane leaped to her feet, her mind dispensing rapid-fire reminders. *Incontinence. Hallucinations. Hostility. If you survive.* Panic set in, deluging her veins with fire and ice. What should she do? What the heck should she do?! Make herself throw up, just in case? Yes, yes. Better safe than sorry.

Jane tore off her gloves, uncaring about the sweat glistening on her fingers. Deep breath in. "You are a Ladling, a caretaker of the dead, and you can do anything. Even this." So. Down the hatch. Except, though she tried her best, she expelled nothing, merely gagging a couple of times.

The panic worsened. She keyed up Grandma Lily's notes to gloss over suggested precautions. *Come to terms with your impending death. Drink plenty of water.*

Water. Yes! Jane raced for her canteen—and got nothing, not even a drop. Empty. She whimpered. Best go home to die then. Trembling, eyes welling, she strode… jogged… sprinted home to say goodbye to Rolex. The thought of her beloved pet sparked hope. If she survived this journey, she would guzzle gallons of water straight from the faucet. And maybe she'd call 911 along the way. Or Fiona, who'd become her dearest companion after Grandma Lily passed. Or Beau, a childhood friend who'd moved away in elementary school, only to return a few months ago. Or Conrad, who probably resented her by now. He'd recently attempted to initiate a meaningful conversation about their relationship, but she'd bailed faster than a cat in a room of rocking chairs, as Grandma Lily liked to say. For reasons! Amazing ones. The best. Another whimper escaped.

The ten trillion-mile voyage home zapped her of strength at the halfway point, and she tripped to a halt. *Oh no!* Her heart galloped with abandon, thumping against her ribs. Wasn't that a symptom of thorn apple consumption?

What if she died of cardiac arrest?

Huffing for every breath, Jane decided to do it. To notify 911. Except, she paused before pressing the final number. The second she made this call, word would spread throughout town. *Jane Ladling, that weird cemetery girl, is doing drugs with the dead.* No thank you. She'd rather die.

She pulled up Fiona's number instead. Except, once again, she hesitated to dial. The dear woman was a worrier. At sixty-two-years-youngish, the grandmother of two didn't need the added stress. And what if Jane died in the middle of the conversation, huh? Could she truly leave her beloved Fiona with such an atrocious memory?

Beau might be the better choice. Since returning from his last tour of duty, he'd acted as Jane's sidekick, helping her with a murder investigation. Long story. Anyway, he tended to exhibit unflappable calm in all situations. A trait gained from his military training. But...

He might need a break from all things death. Which left Conrad, the prime-cut slab of grade A beefcake. He was her boyfriend, but not really her boyfriend, even though technically he was, in fact, her boyfriend, even though he wasn't truly her boyfriend. Whatever. It made sense in her head.

Except, Conrad the Concerned would insist on calling an ambulance and giving the emergency vehicle a police escort. As a special agent with Georgia Bureau of Homicide, he could do it. What if she experienced incontinence while they were together?

I'm going to pee myself, aren't I? Her heartbeat went nuclear, the organ hammering against her ribs. There was no way—zero, none—she was discussing urinary health with Conrad.

She had to call *someone* for help, though. But who—a laugh exploded from her, and she blinked. A laugh? Here? Now? Then her world tilted. Laughing again, she toppled in the grass, where a huge magnolia tree offered a wealth of shade.

Wow. Such a pretty tree. The only one she'd ever seen with three trunks and a million branches.

"Yo! We've got some things to discuss."

What—who—*what?* Gasping, she scanned the area. No one stood nearby. Had she imagined the distinctly male, rumbly voice? No. No way. "Who said that?" she demanded, only to laugh again. She wasn't standing, yet she was somehow spinning in circles. "Where are you? Show yourself before I bury you."

"Over here, weirdo."

The words, now laced with irritation, resonated behind her.

She twisted this way and that, searching... Her gaze skidded over the three-trunked magnolia, only to zoom back. Hold up. Did she see a *face* in one section of bark?

"Gawking is the cruelest thing you can do to someone, you know." The statement spilled from two wooden lips. "Are you always this rude?"

Her jaw slackened. Yes, the tree was speaking to her. And he thought she was rude. She should probably speak back and give him a better—more accurate—impression of her. "I'm *never* rude sometimes. But are you even a someone?"

He humphed. "I'm more of a someone than you are."

Oh, really? "What's your name then?"

"What's yours?" he retorted.

"I'm Jane." Wasn't she? Suddenly she wasn't sure.

"Wrong." He smirked at her. "You're Regret. Miss Regret Cursed the Fourth."

Well. He wasn't wrong. She *was* cursed. Like all the women in her family, she was fated to lose any man she loved. A fact proven in one generation after another, and the reason she felt so uncertain about her almost-relationship with Conrad.

Jane had never imagined she'd lose him because she died, though. Unless he had a thing for former almost-girlfriends who'd become ghosts? Anything was possible.

She gulped and scooted closer to the tree. Since the ancient ones were lauded for their great wisdom, why not seek some much-needed advice? Considering this guy pushed a hundred, he must have oodles of insight.

"There's this man…" she began, only to giggle. What a funny word. Man. May-an. May-ann-aise. Mayonnaise. Hmmm. A turkey and Cheetos sandwich sounded delightful right now.

"You mean Conrad Hotness Ryan. Yeah, I'm familiar."

Excellent. "Do you know what I should do about him?" Despite all the special agent's smoldering glances and sexy come-ons, despite his calls and texts, she had no idea where things stood with him. After the aborted chat, he'd stopped coming around.

"Of course I know. I understand everything about everyone always."

She waited to hear more, beyond eager. "Well?" she prompted, then smacked her lips. Ugh. Why was her mouth so dry? "What should I do?"

"Get ready, because I'm about to blow your mind. You should do…drum roll please…something. And guess what? If no one comes from the future to stop you, you can be confident that you made the right decision."

Ohhhhh. Yes, yes, yes. She should absolutely, positively do this something of which he spoke. Why hadn't she thought of that before? "What else?" she asked her new friend, dizzier by the moment. "Help me fix my life, wise one."

"Never forget that credit cards are free money."

If only she'd known sooner. "Tell me more."

"Always dwell on your mistakes. The waking up in a cold sweat at two in the morning kind of brooding. That's how you learn to do better."

"Smart." Wait. Stars were falling from the sky and sparkling around her. How wonderful. "More!"

"Take things personally from the start. It'll save time."

"I've *always* wanted to save time." Jane felt as if she was guzzling wisdom by the gallon. Conrad and Beau *must* hear this. Both men struggled with problems of some sort too. So, why not call them?

"Don't reach out to your men," Tree advised. "Reach out to the women they're gonna date."

"Conrad is only allowed to see me." She didn't make the rules; she only enforced them. So. She should probably call the two lovely ladies she'd selected for Beau. Eunice Park and Tatiana "Ana" Irons. Eunice worked... somewhere. Ana worked... somewhere else. Since Jane had attended high school with both women, starting a dialogue wouldn't be weird in the slightest. Although...

"I think Fiona told me to stop calling people when I'm sick," she said, vaguely remembering the conversations that had taken place at various times in her life.

Tree shook its leaves, saying, "You aren't sick, are you? Go ahead. Make the calls."

Duh. She *wasn't* sick. Giddier by the second, Jane focused really, really hard on her cell's contact list, dialed one candidate, then the other. Neither woman answered, so she left a voicemail to remind each one about the previous messages she'd left and how much she would appreciate a response.

Wait! She'd forgotten to mention Beau's amazingness. She left another message. As different bits of information flowed through her brain, she left another and another. She phoned until she'd said everything she had to say about everything.

Satisfied with a job well done, she finally rang Conrad.

Since no one from the future showed up, she knew she'd chosen the correct path. When he, too, ignored her, she left a message.

"Guess what?" she told him. "I didn't do any drugs, so I don't need to go to the hospital. I'm not even having problems with my bladder. My panties are bone dry, thank you very much. But do you still want to go on a double date with Beau and his date of my choice or not? If the curse has already driven you away, just tell me already. But do it after the double date. And wear black. It really makes your backside pop. Okay bye."

Nailed it. She dropped the phone and stretched out on the carpet of soft green grass. For minutes, hours or years, she watched as leaves and limbs swayed in the breeze, morphing into shapes. One shape resembled a shadowy, man-sized cloud so close she could reach out and touch it. Warm. Solid. Then gone.

"Come back," she muttered. It didn't. Oh well. Her eyelids turned as heavy as boulders, sliding shut, and she grinned. Darkness enveloped her before a final thought drifted through her mind. *Life has never been better.*

CHAPTER ONE

"Sift enough dirt, find your gold."
Aurelian Hills, Georgia - Speed Dating Event
7 Matches Made

10 days later

*L*ife had never been worse! Caretaker of the dead, shemertaker.

Jane's temples throbbed as she tidied up the small cottage she'd inhabited most of her life. Bright after-noon sun blazed through the windows, illuminating the dust motes that danced through the air. The living room, her current locale, was her favorite spot. A handmade blanket draped over an orange crushed velvet sofa. Near the hearth, two floral print chairs provided a comfy place for her and Fiona to knit toys for children in need.

As she bent over to rearrange the array of throw pillows,

the temple-throbbing worsened, and she groaned. When would the effects of the thorn apple fade?

While the headaches had ebbed and flowed, her dry mouth remained constant. A racing heart kept her tossing and turning every night. Although, yes, the speedy pace might stem from recollections of how she'd behaved while under the influence. What she recalled, anyway. She shuddered to consider the horrors she might have forgotten, her cheeks blazing white-hot with mortification.

Sighing, she dragged a rag over the coffee table. The piece of furniture she treasured most, despite its plethora of nicks. Or maybe because of them. Each mark revived a cherished childhood memory with Grandma Lily, Pops and Fiona. Not to mention the light ring that reminded her of a time she'd been so enraptured by Conrad, she'd set his glass of sweet tea next to the coaster.

Gah! Not again. There was no booting from her mind the man or the messages she'd left for him. Though he had returned her calls the next day, she had refused to pick up. Her usual MO when it came to dealing with her assortment of unsolicited messages. A girl needed time to process her mistakes and prepare for the consequences.

She'd also avoided Beau whenever he'd patrolled the cemetery grounds, doing security things. Whatever that entailed. Thankfully, Eunice and Ana hadn't gotten back to her. A small mercy. And a huge irritation. What would it take to garner a response from either of her former classmates?

For that matter, why hadn't Ana approached Jane for a quote about the recent murder of Dr. Marcus Hotchkins? The crime had taken place here at the cemetery, and Jane was the one who'd stumbled upon the body. If that wasn't worthy of front-page coverage on the AH Headliner—aka the Heads-Up, an app run by the town's only investigative reporter, Ana herself—well, Jane didn't know what was.

Anyway. When she had confessed her tangle with the devil's snare to Fiona during an impromptu Thursday night knitting session, her dear friend had nearly broken a rib from laughing. Especially at the part where Jane admitted to sleeping in the grass all night, then stumbling home the next morning to dispose of the toxic trash bag. A true walk of shame.

But the worst part? She kind of, sort of... missed Tree. The old magnolia hadn't spoken to her a second time. Not even when she'd paced in front of it, demanding a repeat of his sage advice. Or *any* advice. She didn't recall exactly what he'd said the first go round, only that he'd offered answers for her every dilemma.

The sound of something ripping yanked her into the present. What...where...Jane gasped. Using the sharpest of sharp murder mittens, Rolex clawed the lacy curtains that framed the bay window.

"What are you doing?" she called, horrified. "Stop that!"

He continued, bringing down the wrought iron rod anchored to the wall. The metal and material fell, about to crush or smother him.

"Noooo!" She dropped her rag and dove for her fur-baby. To her immense relief, he darted out of the way in time, safe and sound. In the aftermath, however, the relief morphed into sorrow. Grandma Lily had spent weeks sewing those curtains *after* spending years of searching for "the world's most perfect fabric." Now...

Shredded like paper. Tears burned Jane's eyes. Why, why, why would Rolex do this? They'd been together for two years, and he'd never displayed a destructive streak before.

He jumped on the window's ledge and pawed at the glass, releasing a long, drawn-out yowl. A noise he'd never made. The tiny hairs on the back of her neck prickled. Was something wrong? Was he sick? Injured? *Dying?*

Forget the curtains. Jane rushed to her precious, ready to scoop him up and rush him to Dr. Lopez, the local vet. But just as she leaned down, reaching for the little darling, he jumped to the next windowpane. Her gaze moved past him, the glass, and to her front porch, where a strawberry blonde bun rested against the back of Fiona's rocker. *Oh!* Someone had come for a visit.

To Jane's knowledge, there was only one strawberry blonde in town. Well, only one currently. There used to be two. Caroline Wittington, a physician's assistant, turned cold-blooded killer now rotted in prison for murdering a local doctor. And Ana Irons. Or Tatiana. Or Ana. Miss Irons. Whatever. She was the last SB standing. Had she come to discuss the double date with Beau?

About time. Jane rushed to her bedroom, selected the perfect sunhat, and made her way outside, abandoning cool air conditioning for summer heat. She jumped when the door slammed shut behind her. But Ana didn't. Her former classmate remained slumped in the rocker, unmoving.

Wow. Talk about nerves of steel. "Ana. Tatiana. No, let's just go with Ana, okay? Hi. Hello," Jane said, stopping in front of the chair. "I'm so glad you decided to visit, and I apologize for making you wait. Though generally people ring the doorbell when they'd like to chat."

No response. She frowned and studied her guest. Huge white sunglasses shielded Ana's eyes and matched a loose white tank. Her jaw remained set and slack, her cheeks ashen. Drool glistened at the corners of her mouth, and her head drooped at an odd angle. Her arms hung limply at her sides. Had she fallen asleep?

Jane extended a hand, intending to give the town's "premiere journalist" a little shake, only to freeze before contact. Despite the blazing temperature, a chill skittered over her skin. Ana wore light gray slacks soaked with sweat. Or...

Scalp prickling, Jane reared back. She pressed against the front door, the brim of her hat hitting the glass and tilting. At the same time, the golden knocker dug between her shoulders.

"Ana?" she rasped. Wind kicked up once more, making the hem of her yellow fit and flare dress dance below her knees.

Again, there was no response.

From this vantage point, Jane had an unobstructed view of Ana's right side. Not a single part of her twitched. Not once did her chest rise or fall.

"Is this payback for the one and only time you came over to play and I shut you inside a coffin? Because I had the best intentions, I swear!"

Nothing.

"Ana? Or, um, Tatiana, if you prefer?"

Silence.

Swallowing a barbed lump, Jane adjusted her hat, gathered her courage, and closed the distance once again. One baby step after the other. Finally, she stood before her visitor. Ever intensifying tremors plagued her as she reached out to gently remove Ana's sunglasses.

Any second now, Ana would shout "Gotcha!" and they would laugh. Yes, any second.

A ragged puff of air parted Jane's lips when she glimpsed Ana's eyes. All right. So. Ana probably wasn't asleep or pretending. Her lids were open and fixed, her pupils fully dilated. What's more, her skin had begun to sag, making her bones more prominent.

Jane's stomach lurched. She knew death in all its many stages. Not only had she lived in a cemetery her entire life, but as a teenager she'd shadowed a coroner and apprenticed with the town mortician, Adam Rocha Sr. Ana... Tatiana was most certainly dead. Had probably died within the last hour.

The sight of a corpse had never bothered Jane. How could it? She'd learned to walk among the gravestones of Aurelian Hill's oldest cemetery. Picnicked under the shade of the magnolias that surrounded the mausoleum. Helped escort the bodies of the dearly departed to their final resting place. No, her negative reaction stemmed from the implications of finding a corpse *on her porch*...

Taking a deep breath, she felt for a pulse. Just in case. Fingers crossed Ana wore contacts. But honestly? Jane knew the truth deep down.

Cold skin. Nonexistent heartbeat.

Confirmation.

Poor Ana Irons was indeed dead. But why? What had killed her? The heat? A medical condition? Foul play?

Jane's shoulders slumped. Whatever the answer, this was a bona fide tragedy. Once editor of the school newspaper and lead contributor for the high school yearbook, the über-curious Ana used to question everyone about everything. An endearing quality in Jane's book. The inquisitive beauty would be missed by many. And, honestly, she would have positively vibrated with glee at the thought of covering a story like this. The second death to occur on Jane's property in only a handful of months.

The first had brought Special Agent Conrad Ryan to her door. Both a blessing and a curse. What would this newest demise bring? For that matter, why had Ana visited the Garden of Memories in the first place? And to visit this morning of all mornings—the very day she died? What were the odds?

Rolex continued to paw at the window from inside the house. Her darling watch-cat had sensed trouble long before Jane.

"You are this week's employee of the month," she told him through the glass. "You deserve a raise."

He meowed his agreement.

She anchored her hands on her hips. "You'd think there'd be enough dead bodies here, but someone always wants to add another. Hey! Do you suspect Ana's family dropped her off, hoping to avoid a burial fee?" Hadn't Grandma Lily used to complain about such shenanigans?

Focus, Jay Bird, Grandma Lily's voice chided inside her head. *There's a mystery to solve.*

Right. She should call Sheriff Moore. The old grump had jurisdiction here. Although, he would only turn around and alert Conrad, so, probably better to save everyone a little time and go straight to the source herself. She might be at odds with her special agent, kind of, maybe, possibly, but he cared for her well-being. And his job. Not necessarily in that order. He'd want to know what happened.

So. Yes. She would call him first. After she'd assessed the situation to the best of her ability, of course. He would ask questions. Better to have ready answers.

Jane shifted her weight from the heel of one flat to the other as she slipped into "investigation mode" and scanned the potential crime scene. No one seemed to lurk nearby. No discarded weapon waited in plain sight. Near the rocker, a large designer handbag lay on its side.

Back to the victim. Ana had chosen professional clothing for this visit. Had she come from an early meeting? Or had she dressed for Jane or maybe Beau? Maybe an appointment afterward?

Had Ana worked on a story?

Pensive, Jane studied the body more thoroughly. No obvious injuries. No specks of blood. No bruises or disheveled garments. No foul play?

Ready to answer questions, she withdrew her cell from her pocket, a feature she required for every work dress. She liked to look her best for the cemetery's residents, but also insisted on practicality.

Deep breath in. Out. She dialed Conrad's number.

He answered after the third ring, a bit out of breath. "Hello, Jane." To her surprise, humor tinged his voice.

Had he forgiven her for ignoring him since the thorn apple incident?

Her cheeks flooded with heat as a memory tinged the back of her mind. Had she mentioned her panties to Conrad? "Hello," she shrieked at a much louder volume than intended. Deeper breath in. "I'm sorry to say this is a business call." Better. She'd sounded professional.

"Business? Do tell."

"Well. There's a dead body on my porch."

He cleared his throat. "I need you to repeat that. You didn't just tell me—"

"There's a dead body on my porch, yes."

Silence crackled over the line. With a mix of hope and dread, he asked, "Have you been pulling weeds again?"

"I wish." Then the implication of his question hit, and her cheeks heated. Fiona must have told him what happened because Jane certainly hadn't explained.

"Tell me everything," he said, using his flat, no nonsense special agent-detective tone.

That, she could do. "After my morning rounds, I got busy cleaning the house. You know, straightening, running the sweeper, dusting. *Not* because I needed a distraction from a certain conversation centering around my urinary health or anything." Or dozens of other phone calls she'd made that fateful day. "I prefer clean quarters, that's all. Like any normal person. And this is Scrub Up Saturday. As I toiled over the dusting portion of my chores—"

"Jane," he interjected. "Jump ahead. Tell me about the body."

Right. Now wasn't the time to indulge her tendency to ramble. "It's Ana Irons. I mean Tatiana Irons. Well, Ana to her friends, but we hadn't spoken in years, so I might not qualify as a friend. Though I did try to reconnect with her recently. You know, for our double date. She died before rendering a verdict on my use of her name."

"Jane," he barked. A noise infiltrated the line, and she imagined him jumping to his feet, a rolling chair pitching across the room and bouncing against the wall. "I'll be there in thirty minutes."

Really? "Are you not at your office in Atlanta?"

"I am."

"But that's an hour-long drive. Minimum." And he expected to make it in thirty?

"Today, it's half an hour," he grated, and her chest tightened. "Is Beau there? Or nearby? Either way, go inside and lock your doors. Double check every window. Turn on your alarm and do nothing else."

Okay. Time out. She understood there'd been a death and everything, but telling her what to do in her own home? "I don't think—"

"That's right. Don't think. Just do as ordered. I'll contact Sheriff Moore. Expect him within the next fifteen minutes. If not him, someone else. *Is* Beau there?" he asked again.

"No." Some of her irritation faded. This man was majorly concerned for her.

"Call him," he ordered. "And Jane?"

"Yes?"

"I meant what I said. Do nothing else. Under no circumstances are you to launch an investigation." *Click.*

Argh! He'd hung up before she could explain how she'd already begun. And that she planned to continue. In fact, why not gather every bit of possible evidence while she had the chance? During the last investigation, she'd been left out of

this mean the murderer was a female? Or a married man thinking to blame a woman?

Tick, tock.

Now wasn't the time for theories. Jane upended the contents of the bag and hastily collected more pictures. Cherry flavored lip balm. A notepad with a list of numbered nicknames, maybe. A pen with "Manor on Prospect Street" etched into its side. A plastic bag filled with small "cold brew" coffee pods. A small golden shovel with a jagged end, the words "Digging for Gold" stamped on the bottom. A car keypad. A book from the Yellow Brick Abode Library titled *All Write Already*. Three ketchup packets from Old School Burgers. A pair of lacy black underwear in a plastic bag the same size and brand as the other. A melted chocolate bar. A coupon for a "super duper discount" at the Très Chic Consignment. A ticket to the Gold Rush Museum. A mini hammer with FD branded in the handle. And six barrettes.

No cell phone?

Had the killer used the journalist's pale blue Volkswagen Beetle to drop her off? Or was she driven here and killed upon arrival? The automobile could be parked anywhere from the lot to the former office building on the other side of the property. Jane made a mental note to check the security feed. Wait. Security—

Gravel crunched, signaling the approach of a vehicle. Uh-oh. Using her forearm, she swiped everything into Ana's purse and repositioned it exactly how she'd found it. Then, Jane straightened. *Nothing to see here.*

The cleaning gloves! She ripped off and stuffed the latex in her pocket just as Sheriff Moore cut the engine and emerged from his sedan. The soon-to-retire (single) grandfather of eight possessed a thick silver beard, broad shoulders, and a barrel chest. His bald head glistened in the sunlight.

Fiona crushed on him so *hard*.

He marched over, his eyes narrowing on Ana before zooming to Jane. "You draw trouble like a magnet. You know that, right?"

She heaved a sigh. "If I didn't before, I do now."

CHAPTER TWO

"Love. Only faster."
Romance, Arkansas - Bachelor Buffet
3 Matches Made

*W*ithin the hour, policemen, firemen, first responders, the coroner, and special agents overran the Garden of Memories. A familiar situation. Crime scene tape blocked one side of the porch, ruining the country-chic aesthetic.

Jane offered everyone coffee and cream, iced water, sweet tea, and fresh squeezed orange juice. Even the firemen—but they didn't get a smile of welcome with their drink. Her ex-boyfriend was among their number, and whatever he'd said about her ensured no one had the courage to meet her gaze. Not that she cared. Not even a little.

Hours passed. Finally, one group after another took off, until only a single team of expert investigators remained. But they stayed forever. All day, in fact. They traipsed all over, snagging pictures and samples of everything. Sometimes, someone knocked on the door to ask her questions. So many questions she couldn't remember them all. Or even one. At some point, they asked to see her hands.

Conrad never showed. By late afternoon, she grew worried about him. Whenever her confusion, concern or frustration ballooned, she ventured outside to offer more refreshments and slip in a query of her own. Namely where Special Agent Ryan happened to be. Each time, she received the same, non-helpful response.

"I'm not sure, ma'am. If you'll excuse me."

Ma'am. As if she sported mom jeans or something.

The agents left shortly after midnight. Still, she received no calls, texts, or visits from Conrad. Beau and Fiona called and texted a thousand times, checking on her. Apparently, Conrad *had* called them and commanded them to stay away from the cemetery until tomorrow. Which meant, yes, Jane worried throughout the night, alone save for Rolex, tossing and turning.

Just as the sun dawned, both Beau and Fiona arrived. Thank goodness! The handsome former soldier dazzled in a plain white T-shirt and worn jeans. Fiona wore her usual fare: a blouse with a dizzying array of colors, loose slacks that never matched, and a chunky necklace made by her daughter.

"Have you heard anything else from Conrad?" she asked as they settled on opposite sides of the couch.

"Not a peep," Fiona replied. At the same time, Beau shook his head and announced, "Nope."

Jane's frustration transformed into irritation. Wringing her hands, she paced in her living room. Was Conrad okay? Had something happened to him? To ignore her like this, after what had transpired… *He better be dead!*

Rolex perched on the coffee table in front of Beau, hissing periodically. Every so often, he glanced up from his cell phone to acknowledge her cat's efforts to terrify him with a muttered, "Keep trying. I almost trembled that time."

Rolex hated all males, but he despised Conrad most of all. Her sweet, adorable little feline protector dreamed of clawing her smoldering, kinda sorta still-in-negotiations-about-it boyfriend. He must fear Conrad would win her heart, displacing him.

Well, Conrad would not be winning anything. First of all, nothing and no one could steal her affections from her fur-baby. Second, Jane wasn't interested in loving and losing the agent. He was lucky she'd let herself fall into like with him.

He—argh! People were trampling her carefully manicured carpets of grass again. Messing up her flowers. Disturbing the birds. Dang it! Where was Conrad? Why hadn't he arrived as promised, or at least called?

"Worrying isn't going to help the situation, hon," Fiona told her. The petite, curvy widow had a short cap of black and gray curls, and lovely dark skin. The fine lines around her rich brown eyes came courtesy of love and laughter. "You should use your time wisely and fix your drapes. What on earth happened to them?"

"Hurricane Rolex. And I'm not worrying," Jane replied. "I'm steaming! Forget Conrad. Someone is possibly trying to frame me for murder."

"Steaming won't help the situation either." Beau was a big man. Tall and muscular, with a mop of blond waves and vivid green eyes. The scent of pine and soap always wafted from him, his softest feature. A true comfort to Jane. He peered down at his phone, a frown pulling at the corners of his mouth.

"Are you searching for a home?" she asked, pacing faster. He'd been living at a nearby motel, often turning down her offer of the guest room. Something she hated with the heat of a thousand suns. He was a sensitive soul, and he needed—deserved—a home. If he didn't find a decent dwelling by week's end, Jane planned to start sneaking house listings into his truck.

"I found a place on Prospect Street for Peach State Security, with an apartment overhead for me. I move in a few days, maybe a week or so. Depends on when the contractors finish with some updates."

Prospect Street. Wow. The fancy part of town. "That's wonderful. Why don't I throw you a housewarming party?"

"No, thank you. Now sit down and let the agents do their jobs. You're innocent. You've done nothing...wrong," he finished, radiating bafflement.

"You're right. Of course you're right." Plus, he'd recently installed infrared cameras around the outside of the house, the different areas of the cemetery and each of the gardens.

Which an agent had asked for. Twice. Jane had panicked and blurted out, "I need to speak with my lawyer." She had done something wrong–and she had been filmed doing it.

"I have some military friends coming to town at some point," he said, frowning at his screen. "They served in my unit. They're considering moving here and working with me. I'll brief them on the situation when they arrive, if you're agreeable, and we'll put them to work patrolling the grounds for a while. Make sure no other corpses show up."

"Certainly," she managed to eke out. "I need to speak with you about something. You see, the agents want our camera feed. But—"

"You rifled through Ana's pockets?" he demanded, his gaze flipping up. "And her purse?"

How did he already—her eyes widened. He was going over the video *now*. As the chief security officer here, he had total access. So. She should have known. "I, um. Well. I kind of forgot the cameras were recording." A mistake anyone could have made. Including the killer! "Did you not go over the feed yesterday?"

"I did not. I was busy tracing a hacker. Someone tapped into the footage. I've been working to find out who, and if they tampered with anything."

Jane gasped. "The killer did it." Because there was no such thing as a coincidence. The violation left her quaking with rage.

Fiona tsk-tsked. "Let's back up a second. Jane, you searched the murder victim?"

"Um...well..."

"I'm *so* disappointed in you." Her friend gave her a mournful shake of her head. "You had plenty of time to tell me everything you found and you didn't."

"Do you want to see the pictures?" She reached for her phone.

"Don't." Beau glared at Jane, then Fiona, then back to Jane. "Not while the agents are here."

She winced and wrung her hands. "Speaking of the agents, I basically asked for a lawyer during our last conversation."

"That's not a bad thing," he said. "Always err on the side of caution."

"Should she give the security feed to Conrad?" Fiona asked. "She might have searched Ana's things, but she certainly didn't kill the girl."

He shook his head. "No. Give me a little more time with it."

Jane met Beau's gaze. "Did you happen to see who brought Ana to the porch?"

"She walked by herself."

What? "You're joking." Hurrying over, Jane plopped down at his side and snatched the phone. "Let me see."

With a press of a few buttons and Ana appeared on the

screen, stumbling to the porch, seeming to talk to someone who wasn't there. She tripped and crashed next to the window, then fell into the rocker, all without making a peep.

"She was most likely drunk?" Or high. "There was no foul play?"

"Let's hope." He scrubbed a hand over his face. "When Conrad asks, and he will, you checked her for signs of life. Say nothing else. Do you understand?"

What was with the men in her sphere, always bossing her around? "Well, I really don't need to say anything else because that isn't a lie... exactly." She bit her bottom lip. A ridiculous nervous habit she'd developed during the last case. "For all I knew, Ana had a lifesaving inhaler or EpiPen she desperately needed."

Another car pulled up and parked in the drive, visible through the window.

"Conrad!" She spotted him as he stepped from the familiar sedan. Finally!

She jumped up, tossing her friend his phone, and rushed over to flatten her palm on the pane of glass. Her heart thudded as she looked him over. Conrad was as tall and muscular as Beau, with hair so black it gleamed blue in the sunlight. A prominent brow, strong nose and bronze skin only added to his appeal. The dark shadow dusting his jaw hinted at a sleepless night and a rough morning.

He wore a tailored suit and tie, just like the one he'd sported the first day they'd met, and he was so handsome he stole her breath. Sunglasses shielded intense amber eyes, but she sensed the moment he'd spotted her and their gazes locked. But all too soon, he offered her a stiff nod and turned to speak to someone else. His partner, Special Agent Tim Barrow, an older man with salt and pepper hair, skin weathered by the sun and a prominent belly. He'd all but paced across the porch since his arrival bright and early this morning. He too was dressed exactly as before: a blue, collared shirt with khakis.

Her stomach twisted with nerves. Neither man ventured inside the house. Instead, they spoke with a woman who then strode to the porch and knocked on the front door.

Uh-oh. This couldn't be good. Dreams of no foul play crashed and burned.

Jane shoved today's hat on her head, even though she planned to remain indoors. Deep breath in. Out. Okay. A measure of calm settled over her. *Let's do this.*

She opened the entrance, old hinges creaking. "Yes!" Whoa. Too forceful. Almost guilty. She pasted on a bright smile. "Hello. I'm Jane Ladling, the owner and operator of Garden of Memories, where your loved ones rest in beauty as well as peace." The company motto slipped out, exactly as it had done the day she'd met Conrad and Agent Barrow. "I'm the one who found the body. How may I help you?"

"I'm Agent Hightower. I'd like to ask you a few questions. May I come in?"

"Of course. Yep. I have no problems with that. No reason to refuse." Did she? Jane awkwardly stepped aside, allowing the investigator to enter.

The other woman towered over Jane's five-five frame, exactly as that last name promised. Very pretty and probably in her mid-thirties, with dark hair cut in an inverted bob that complimented strong features. The straightness of her shoulders made her almost regal.

Jane didn't mean to, but nerves got the better of her. "I'm Jane, by the way." Wait. They'd covered that earlier. The silence was getting to her, that was all. "Please, sit anywhere you'd like. No one bites. Except Rolex. He's already plotted to kill you eighteen different ways." *Seriously. Shut up.* "Not that murder is always on his mind. Or mine."

Rolex swiped his paws at the newcomer as she settled in a

chair at the hearth and withdrew a small notebook and pen. Jane eased into the seat across from her, missing her own investigative pad. A little blue beauty she'd named *Truth Be Told*.

"Will Conrad–I mean, Special Agent Ryan–be joining us today?" she asked, doing a bang-up job of hiding her eagerness.

"No."

She offered no other words, and Jane deflated. Did that mean the higher ups already considered Jane a suspect, and this was to be a full-on interrogation?

"I know you suffered quite a shock yesterday, Miss Ladling, and you'd probably like to be left alone. But additional questions have arisen. I promise I'll be as gentle as I can, but I must ask you some difficult things."

"I understand." And she did. "I have additional questions too. Was a horrible crime committed, or was this an accident?"

"Miss Irons was murdered."

Well. *Everyone* deflated.

Pen at the ready, Hightower said, "Tell me how you discovered the body."

Her statement. Again. Was the would-be interrogator double-checking to try and catch Jane in a lie?

She sighed and told the newcomer exactly what she'd told the others.

For over an hour, Hightower peppered Jane with questions. Everything from her movements over the past week to her thoughts of Ana in high school. Jane offered the truth. It set you free every single time; maybe not at first, but definitely later. Lies only ever led to more trouble. But then Hightower asked her next question...

"How long has jimsonweed grown on your property?"

"Oh. You mean the thorn apple?" She frowned. "What has

that to do with anything?" Had Conrad mentioned it to his coworkers? But why would he do so?

Someone pounded on the door. Two crisp raps Jane immediately recognized. Gasping, she popped to her feet.

Conrad didn't wait for permission to enter. He stalked inside, paused in the foyer and frowned. When the scent of dry ceded and refined spice hit, she shivered. That he'd rolled up his sleeves, displaying tattooed forearms and a Rolex, only amplified her reaction.

His posture was stiff as a board as he scanned… His eyes stopped on Jane and narrowed. "This interview is over."

"Actually, it's only getting started." Hightower jerked to her feet. "I doubt you've forgotten this is *my* investigation, Special Agent Ryan."

"I've just been informed Miss Ladling has asked for a lawyer. Twice. You know the rules as well as I do, yes?" His tone was as hard as his knock and as rough as his palms. He shifted his grim energy to Jane. "Have your lawyer call Hightower ASAP."

"But I didn't do anything wrong." Well, not more than a few things.

Hightower pursed her lips, but kept her attention on Jane, who got busy adjusting the brim of her hat. "You can help me prove your innocence with a copy of your security feed."

"I'm happy to send you what's available," Beau answered on her behalf. He, too, stood. "As soon as you show me a warrant."

The agent worked her jaw before she nodded and dug out her card. "Here's my contact information. I suggest you use it. Soon."

Jane gulped. Okay. That had escalated quickly.

~

JANE TOOK Conrad's advice and hired a lawyer that very day. The only one she could afford—Anthony "Tony" Miller. The guy wasn't her biggest fan. Not too long ago, she'd accused him of cold-blooded murder, putting him in GBH's headlights, helping solidify his divorce to Emma Miller, another suspect.

She eased into a plush leather chair, placed her purse atop her thighs, adjusted her hat—yes, she still wore it—and scanned the office. A match to Tony himself. The two existed in total disarray. Papers were scattered here and there. Notebooks, files, and pens stacked on each side of his desk. Coffee stains on the computer keyboard.

He gulped three fingers of scotch and laughed. "Let me get this straight." He was an attractive enough guy with gray-streaked hair and an unkempt beard. But strain etched his mouth, his very presence seeming to suck energy from the room. His wrinkled shirt lacked a middle button. "You scheduled this meeting because you were dumb enough to handle a dead body, which the cops might or might not know, and you expect me to keep you out of jail either way." Ice cubes clinked as he slammed the glass to his desk. "Why would I ever do that?"

"Because I'm a paying customer. Which means you need me as much as I need you. I've heard the rumors. You are losing clients left and right." Truth was truth. And since she had to oh, so often take it, she had earned the privilege to dish it. "I figure your rates must be at level desperate now."

He stiffened. "You did not call me desperate."

His tone was so low and menacing, Jane might have feared for her life if she'd been alone. Well, probably not 'feared.' She could deliver a mean left hook when warranted. Just ask Tony's soon to be ex-wife. But there was no need for even the slightest twinge of worry now. Beau sat at her side, a tower of strength and menace. No one dared threaten her when he guarded her. And guard her, he did.

After Conrad had advised her to hire a lawyer, Beau had sprung into action. He'd helped Jane and Fiona print and study each of the crime scene photos. They needed to know what had caused Conrad to react so strongly, so the launch of their investigation and the creation of their new club— Team Truth—had begun.

They'd learned a lot of valuable information. Namely, Ana had suspected everyone in town of every kind of crime imaginable. Affairs. Thefts. Illicit favors. Secret societies. Secret babies. Switched at birth babies. Hidden treasures. Family wars. Speed dating scandals. Jane remained mind boggled by it all. She hadn't fit any puzzles pieces together, so she didn't know who'd done what. But she would. Soon. Someone might have killed Ana to keep their secrets secret.

The photos of Ana's notepad. The list of nicknames, most linked to a line of numbers. Dates, maybe. Probably. Jane noted the stars next to "Dr. Sexy Evil" "Art Amour" and "The Robber." On the last page, the would-be journalist had written and circled the words *Speed dating. My big break?*

Uh, why was Tony glaring at her, silent?

Oh, right. He'd asked a question. "No, I most certainly did not call you desperate," Jane said and sighed, jumping back into the conversation. "I called your rates desperate. There's a difference."

He swiped his tongue over his teeth, and she heaved another sigh, hating the need to be here. What had the agents found on her property? What had turned her into a prime person of interest when there was a wealth of others to go around? Why had Hightower asked about the jimsonweed? And how did someone hacking into the cemetery's security feed figure into things—because it must?

"Discounted rate, discounted services," he finally muttered.

"Jane," Beau said, even while offering a cold smile to the other man. "Why don't you explain to good ole Tony that he'll work for the money as if his very life depends on it?"

"Oh. Well. Yes." She cleared her throat. "I need you to help me prove my innocence, Tony."

"Mr. Miller," he corrected, flashing a toothy smile-nonsmile.

Whatever. "I'm a single cat mom, and I'm unwilling to go to jail until Rolex is dead. And he's never going to die." His hatred for humanity would pickle him and cause him to live forever.

"No one is going to jail," Beau remarked, his irritation clear. His temper remained on a short fuse today.

She reached over and patted his hand.

Tony—Mr. Miller—ugh, no, she'd stick with Tony. It was too late to change the way she thought of him. Anyway. He scrubbed a palm over his face before grabbing the crystal decanter on his desk and refilling his glass, grumbling, "What does it matter? I'll take the case."

He would? "Oh, that's wonderful! Thank you." She grinned and clapped. Then frowned. Why had he given in so easily? The guy wasn't her biggest fan. And he'd just agreed to accept an obscenely low paycheck. What if... no, no. He wouldn't dare.

Unless he would.

No. No way. Tony hadn't arranged Ana's death simply to strike at Jane.

Unless he had. He did bear a major grudge against Jane. How best to hurt her than to frame her for murder? And what could be more satisfying than tricking her into hiring the actual murderer to defend her?

Well, more reason to hire him then! What better way to study him and learn his motives?

Or he was simply a halfway decent guy under a tremendous amount of stress because his marriage had just fallen apart.

"Tell me again. What happened? Start with the thorn apple," Tony requested, leaning against his seat, and linking his hands over his middle.

Like Hightower, he questioned her for over an hour. After tossing back another glass of scotch, he sat up. "All right. I'm ready." Spine ramrod straight, he lifted the agent's business card and dialed the number.

Jane perched at the edge of her seat during the entire conversation, clutching Beau's hand. The sweet guy let her do it, never complaining.

Tony asked the agent far more questions than he answered, his expression unchanging. His aggravated tone never faltered. After hanging up, he exhaled a heavy breath, dosing the air with the pungent sting of alcohol. He appeared more stressed than ever, but also weary.

"Well?" she demanded, nearly snapping Beau's bones. Still, he didn't complain.

"You go in for questioning in two hours," Tony stated. "They have questions about a series of bizarre voicemail messages."

Oh...no.

CHAPTER THREE

"Meet and repeat!"
Love, Texas - Meet 'n Greet
1 Match Made

*J*ane and Tony sat on one side of a cold metal table, with Agent Hightower and Special Agent Barrow on the other. The small, sterile "interview" room boasted only the table and a camera. Its glass eye glared malice at her.

Conrad stood behind the two-way mirror, she just knew it. His searing gaze had already burned two holes in her brow. She straightened in the uncomfortable crossback chair and fiddled with the angle of her hat. Surely, he believed in her innocence.

"Remind me what happened with the jimsonweed," Hightower said, making her jump.

The agent offered the words like a suggestion, an invitation, but Jane knew she'd just received a command. So far, she'd been forced to outline the day's events twice and explain the thorn apple thrice.

Suspicions danced at the back of her mind. On the camera feed, Ana had seemed drunk or high. What if she'd been drugged by her killer?

"Well," Jane began, and cleared her throat.

"No," Tony burst out, silencing her. He banged a fist on the table, all drama and flare. Was he trying to impress someone? "She's done explaining the weed. Move on."

She glanced at her lawyer, impressed by his vehemence on her behalf. Maybe he didn't hate her after all.

Wait, how silly of her. Of course, he hated her. He simply adored her payment.

Hightower appeared none too happy with the refusal, but she nodded. "Very well. Why don't we listen to the messages you left for Miss Irons?"

Must we?

Jane didn't remember exactly what she'd said, but it couldn't be *that* bad. Right?

Please be right.

Suddenly her frenzied, manic voice spilled from a speaker. "Hi! Hello. This is Jane. Jane Eleanor Ladling. The cemetery girl. I just wanted to touch base with you. Remember our double date? I mean, I know you haven't agreed to go or anything, but you will. Or else." She laughed with diabolical glee. "I kid, I kid. You'll agree just as soon as I tell you how wonderful Beau is. So wonderful! Call me back for once. Or else. I might be serious this time. This is Jane."

She cringed. Okay, not the greatest start, but not the worst either. Based on what she'd been told of her messages to Fiona and Beau, it could have been a whirlwind of awful.

Then another message played. "Hi, Ana. Or Tatiana. Jane here. I just figured it out. You're ignoring me because you're afraid of death. I'm right, aren't you? But there's no reason to fear. I'll work hard to make it a beautiful experience for you, promise. You'll swear you're almost alive. Okay. Bye."

Her lawyer hissed air between his teeth. Nice game face. But yeah, she kind of understood why her innocent messages had drawn unnecessary attention.

Rolling into the next, Jane's laughter rang out. "Yo! Ana banana. Who still believes in Santa! Who lives with her nana. Oh, I forgot. You hated that in the third grade. Oops. Sorry. Guess what? You should always listen to the tree people. They are never wrong. Oh, wow. How'd this cool sword get into my hand? Tick tock."

And the next. "—be honest, okay? Is Conrad as hot as I think he is? Or is he hotter? Dang! He's hotter, isn't he? He's gonna break my heart, and the curse is gonna win again. No, don't try to make me feel better. Let me drown in my ocean of misery. Okay, bye!"

She would not look at the two-way mirror.

And the next. "Greetings. I still haven't met me from the future, which means this is a great idea. Unless I died. Do you think I died? Okay, bye!"

A click sounded, ending the call, before her voice echoed, the recording seamlessly flowing into another.

"All treefolk should be chopped down immediately. Off with their heads!"

"Ana! It's Jane. Get this. I just had a brilliant idea." Sudden silence. "What? No! Shhh. Be quiet. I'm talking to someone special." Another beat without her drunker and drunker sounding voice. "So? What do you say? Ana? Hello? Are you still not there?"

Oh, no, no, no. Jane's hands grew clammy. Sweat dampened the back of her neck. Thank goodness for the shadows the hat cast over her burning cheeks.

"This last one is my favorite," Hightower said with a gotcha twinge.

The final recording began. "'Member when we were kids, and you came over that one time and we played hide and seek in the gardens 'cause I wanted to host your funeral *so bad*. I still do. What do you say? Can I?"

Jane barely stifled the urge to groan. "I did not kill Ana. But if I had, I could have easily hidden her body. No one would have ever known."

"I believe you," Hightower encouraged. "Please explain how you would have done the hiding, so we can prove your innocence."

Tony gripped her arm to silence her.

"Why would I call the cops if I did the deed?" Jane demanded against the non-verbalized advice of her legal counsel.

"Bragging rights. Fun and games. Fame. A way to point to your supposed innocence. A boost in finances. Your business runs on a slim trust, and the previous murder brought in a multitude of paying customers, did it not?" Barrow asked, speaking up for the first time. "Maybe you hoped to cash in on another homicide."

Yeah. All right. Those were seriously good reasons.

"Maybe you hoped to host Miss Irons' funeral," Hightower said, going for a gentler approach now. "Maybe it was an accident. Maybe you got angry when she failed to respond to you, and you decided to force the matter. Whatever happened, it's clear you regret it now. You aren't a bad person, Jane. That much is clear. You're scared. And I get it. Just tell us what occurred, and we'll do what we can to help you."

Jane's lips parted. "I *have* told you what occurred. Many times. You refuse to believe me."

"You know what? We're done here." Tony stood, sending his chair sliding across the cheap linoleum floor. More drama. "My client has already admitted to leaving those messages when she was under the accidental influence of jimsonweed, thorn apple, locoweed—whatever you want to call it. Something no one in their right mind would have done. She's been nothing but cooperative with you, offering up her home and business, answering the same questions multiple times. This is bordering on harassment."

Yes! Harassment. But had he really needed to use the description "no one in their right mind?"

Hightower motioned to the discarded seat with a clipped wave. "Sit down, Mr. Miller. We aren't done here."

"Like I said, we *are* done here." Tony leaned over the table, flattening his palms over the surface and drumming his fingers. *Tap, tap, tap.* "Either charge my client or we walk."

Wait. What? *Charge* her? The moisture in Jane's mouth dried. Should he be taunting the agents like this?

A double rap sounded at the door. Conrad entered with a clipped gait, his suit wrinkled for the first time since they'd met. A five o'clock shadow dusted his jaw, and lines of fatigue fanned his eyes. Had he gotten any sleep since the murder?

Avoiding Jane's gaze, he set a laptop at the edge of the table, with the screen facing toward the other investigators. "Beauregard Harden emailed the security footage."

Her shoulders tensed and her stomach churned because she knew what the video feed would showcase. She might end up charged with a crime, after all.

"Let it be noted my client handed over the footage voluntarily," Tony announced.

Except, Beau had mentioned a warrant. Why, why, why hadn't he waited for it?

One charge for obstruction, coming up.

Special Agent Barrow smashed the play button with a meaty finger. A multiview image of the cemetery filled the screen. The porch. The grounds. The work shed.

The flash of pale blue caught her attention. Jane squirmed as she watched Ana Irons practically fall out of her Volkswagen Beetle and stagger through the Garden of Memories entrance. The redhead wobbled along the cobblestone paths, lurching, and nearly toppling, the security system's eagle eye capturing her every move. Finally, she stumbled to the porch, dropping her purse at her feet, and collapsing into the rocking chair, leaving a hunk of her hair in the nail on the windowpane.

Jane studied her face during the fall. Ana never even flinched. Dead woman walking.

The next few minutes of feed offered nothing but the breeze, dancing strands of hair and a visit from a humming-bird stopping by the porch feeder for a quick snack. Then the curtain in the window began to ruffle. Rolex appeared. Moments later, Jane rushed onto the porch, flying into action. She removed Ana's sunglasses. Then she called Conrad.

Jane ground her back molars. She knew what everyone would see next. *Me, rifling through Ana's pockets and purse.* Snapping photos of a dead body like a murder obsessed weirdo. Except...

...the screen blurred as the motion-detecting camera shifted focus away from the porch to something else. No, not something. A cat. *Her* cat. Rolex perched in the living room window, situated between drapes, tilting his head this way and that as he peered out the glass. For the next few moments, she saw nothing but her miniature house panther with a face meant to top the list of the world's most adorable animals in history or imagination. But, but...

What? She distinctly remembered those drapes being *on the floor* at the time of Ana's death. Had Beau altered the footage? Oh, dang. He had, hadn't he? He'd committed a crime for her.

Stay calm. Give nothing away. For your sake and for Beau's.

What must Conrad be thinking? She chanced a glance at

him under her lashes. His focus remained on the investigators. Gauging their reactions?

"It appears Miss Irons died before Miss Ladling ever showed up," Tony said with a smirk, pulling Jane to her feet. "We're leaving." He arched a brow at Hightower. "Unless you have anything else to add?"

Conrad looked between the lawyer and Jane, though his gaze did not linger on her. "Lab results are in. Cause of death is jimsonweed poisoning via Miss Iron's morning coffee."

Jane sucked in a breath. She remembered seeing the small coffee pods in Ana's purse. But how had the journalist not tasted or smelled the thorn apple?

"An accidental death then, I'm sure." Tony bent to pick up his briefcase. "My client is an example of how easily the substance can be misused."

"All I'm hearing is conjecture," Hightower countered. "Here are the facts. Miss Ladling grew the plant on her property. The same strain that killed Miss Irons. Yes, we found the trash bag of stalks Miss Ladling tossed out ten days before the victim died."

The same strain? Seriously?

"Something else my client explained. She got rid of something able to poison her pet." Faux humor tugged at the lawyer's lips. "Besides, does my client look like someone able to plot and scheme that far in advance?"

That was meant to be an insult, right? Jane bit the inside of her lip and held her tongue. He was either playing a role or getting his digs in while he could.

Tony responded to his own question with a throaty chuckle that seemed to burrow under Hightower's skin. Two rosy spots popped on her cheeks. "Jimsonweed is common enough. It isn't even illegal here. Last year it was found in the city's park. Should you arrest the mayor? The city council has a few dubious characters in it. Maybe start there," he suggested, the words thick with sarcasm.

He appeared to know an awful lot about the weed. Too much?

Hightower stood, not a strand of her bob ruffled, but oh, the heat in her eyes could melt a pair of handcuffs. Jewelry Jane might be sporting soon if her lawyer didn't stop taunting the woman who seemed determined to put her behind bars.

"Let's consider the timeline," Jane said. "When I was tripping on thorn apple, I experienced the side-effects twenty minutes—"

"No, not another word from you. Let's go." With a hand on her elbow, Tony helped her to her feet.

Argh! She'd wanted to ask if the GBH knew where Ana had come from before she'd arrived at the cemetery.

None of the agents tried to stop her as Tony led her toward the door. Jane avoided Conrad's gaze as she passed him, not ready for another glimpse of his impassive expression. As Tony escorted her through the station, she remained quiet, pensive.

Why had Ana even come to the Garden? Why had she written Jane's name on a piece of paper, as if she needed help recalling it? Why had the thorn apple grown in the first place? Especially in a section of the cemetery without cameras. And only appearing ten days before Ana's arrival, as Hightower had pointed out. Ana, who'd been high on the same strain. The timing and coincidence of everything struck Jane as highly questionable.

She thought back to the day she'd found the thorn apple. Had she missed or forgotten anything important? She remembered speaking with the tree. Remembered...something else. It teased the periphery of her thoughts...oh! The cloud. She recalled seeing a man-shaped cloud. On the ground.

She frowned. A figment of her imagination or an actual human? The one who'd planted the weed, perhaps? She concentrated on the image, hoping to gain an idea of size, but dang it, she recalled nothing but a blur.

Tony's question offered insight, at least. *Does my client look like someone who is able to plot and scheme that far in advance?*

Jane might not have plotted anything in advance, but someone else clearly had. And that someone had gone to great lengths to spotlight her supposed guilt.

"Miss Ladling," Conrad called from behind her.

She spun, her heart racing. "Yes?"

For the first time since this whole ordeal started, he held her gaze. His amber eyes crackled with heat. "You forgot your purse." He handed the bag over, his fingers purposely brushing hers.

Shivers of warmth and relief loosened the tightness between her shoulder blades. He didn't blame her for the crime. And he would come for her as soon as they caught the killer. That, she suddenly knew, beyond any doubt.

She smiled and softly told him, "Good day to you, Officer Detective Special Agent Ryan."

"Good day to you, Miss Ladling. I'll be seeing you real soon. That's a promise."

∼

DAY one after her interrogation passed without word from Conrad.

Day two flew by with zero phone calls or texts.

Same with days three, four and five. Jane knew what that meant. The real killer had yet to be unearthed. Not that she had idled by her phone, doing nothing. Jane visited Beau's swanky new place and cooked him a nice dinner to celebrate his first night there. Mostly she studied Ana's notes as if it were a million dollar an hour job. She also revisited the Valley of the Dolls, home of the unforgettable thorn apple. Or rather, the devil's snare. Yes, that name was a far better fit.

The weed absolutely lived up to its name, ensnaring her in a whole heap of trouble. More and more, she was certain it had been purposely planted to point to her guilt. The timing, the location, the consequences–calculated and intentional. Also, the way the roots had lifted so easily from the earth bothered her. As if the taps and shoots weren't yet fully threaded, despite the abundance of growth.

The killer was smart. And evil. But who in the world was evil enough to do a despicable thing like this?

Well. Honestly? Lots of people. In fact, the list lengthened when she settled on the living room couch to pore through Ana's notes once again. Wow. Just wow. While some of the town's people had accused Jane of having an overactive imagination filled with wild allegations and theories, Ana had distrusted everyone at gold medal Olympic levels.

How could the mayor give lucrative city contracts to his cousin?

Was Sheriff Moore's deputy truly gambling online while clocked in for duty?

And just where did all the copy paper for Aurelian Hills Elementary end up?

Jane settled more comfortably against the cushions and forced herself to focus on the list of sixteen nicknames and numbers, with Ana's final note like a neon sign in the back of her mind: *Speed dating. My big break?* A cup of chamomile tea liberally doused with honey steamed on the coffee table. Grandma Lily's orange blanket draped her legs, and a laptop perched on her lap.

Hours passed as Jane scoured pages on the Headliner, hoping to link citizens of the town with a nickname or date. No real luck. When her vision blurred, she moved on to the photos she'd taken, hoping to find a link there. But the things she'd found in the victim's pockets revealed nothing. The half a dozen angles of the body...nope.

She sighed. The next set of photos displayed the contents of her purse. Jane zoomed in on the coffee pods. Okay. All right. Now she was getting somewhere. A specialty blend for "extra pops of energy."

After a quick internet search, she placed an order with expedited shipping, despite the added cost. Why not try one and get herself in Ana's headspace for a bit?

With that done, other questions formed. Why had Ana carried around bagged underwear? Evidence of some sort? And what about the little golden shovel? It had a jagged edge, as if it were a... key? Oh, oh yes! A key! That made sense. But what did it unlock? A secret safe deposit box? A room for a secret lover's tryst?

The words etched on the side echoed through her mind. *Digging for gold*. Wait. Hold up. Hadn't she seen the same phrase on the large billboard that advertised the weekly speed dating events in town?

Finally! A connection! Jane's back shot straight. The nicknames and their numbers corresponded with speed dating, Ana's big break, which must correspond with the key.

Well, well, well. Looked like Jane needed to take this investigation out in the world and hit the dating market.

Trembling, she popped to her feet and rushed to the office in the back of the cottage. An addition built by her beloved Pops, the best grandad ever to live, and a place even quirkier than the rest of the property. Corners set at odd angles. Filing cabinets stood in a subtle but zagged line. Framed photos of her favorite people covered the walls. Grandma Lily and Pops, of course. Fiona and Rolex, too. There was even a picture of Jane's mother and father from high school graduation. It hung next to the gilt-framed cross-stitched display of Henry Cavill's perfect face. A garage sale purchase worth far more than the twenty bucks Jane had forked over.

She should probably, maybe, perhaps consider thinking about probably, maybe, perhaps putting up a photo of Conrad and Beau. They were a big part of her life. For now. Really, what would it hurt?

Something to consider later. At the slightly messy antique desk, she threw open her laptop and opened the website for the speed dating venue. *Yes!* Tickets were still available for the event on Saturday. Which meant Jane would attend, along with Beau and Fiona.

Go Team Truth!

CHAPTER FOUR

"Get 'em while they're hot!"
Happyland, Oklahoma - Catch A Mate Night
101 Matches Made!

"Welcome to our Strike it Hitched extravaganza, where you pan for a gold star match. Or two! How can we help you help yourself tonight?"

Jane slapped on a smile and stepped forward. She'd forced herself to attend the event without a hat, even though she'd chosen to wear her flirtiest dress. A knee-length polka dot fit and flare with a lacy collar and hem. The polka dots were little hearts, none the same color.

Fiona and Beau flanked her sides. Both of her friends had taken a different approach with their wardrobe. The sixty-two-year-young grandmother of four had highlighted her curves with a tight black number. On the other hand, Beau had chosen a plain white T-shirt and swim trunks.

Swim trunks.

Oh, whatever. This was too great a day to fuss about her friend's lack of undercover investigative skills. Jane was

49

about to launch her first sting operation. And she adored being inside the Manor on Prospect Street, the fanciest property in town. Seriously. No wonder Ana had carried their pen everywhere she ventured. Once a private home of the richest man in Aurelian Hills, now a glamorous bed-and-breakfast regularly featured on the top ten list of places to visit in Georgia, the Manor boasted luxury at every angle.

The elegant lobby dazzled with a domed ceiling and a massive crystal chandelier, stealing her breath every time she glimpsed it. Murals of gold mines and miners demanded a second and third look. At her feet, gold veined marble gleamed.

Blocking off the entrance to the ballroom was a long, rectangular table, where two forty-something sisters perched, seemingly out of place in T-shirts, jeans, and the brightest lipstick Jane had ever seen. Beyond the pair was a ballroom filled with an array of small, round tables covered in light pink bunting. Rose bouquets acted as centerpieces, saturating the air with sweetness. Heart-shaped candles crackled, all but screaming *romance*.

"Jane." Fiona elbowed her in the side. "Respond to the nice ladies, hon."

Oh. Right. "I'm Jane Ladling," she told the hosts, Charlotte and Audrey Berdize, as brightly as she was able. "I purchased three tickets for tonight's speed dating to love event. Please and thank you."

Fiona, dear woman that she was, had gotten on board Jane's speed dating plan a hundred percent. To catch Ana's killer, they must follow her footsteps. That meant participating in a fake search for love. Or semi-fake. Beau still needed a date. He'd gotten on board with the plan too, though...after only an hour and a half of non-stop persuasion. And a promise to prepare him a home-cooked meal once a week for six months. The entire time she'd outlined the method to her maddening brilliance, his eyes had gleamed with excitement—definitely not horror.

"Jane Ladling?" Charlotte, the older of the gatekeepers, chirped. "Well bless your sweet little heart. We didn't think you'd come."

"We sure didn't," Audrey echoed.

"I'll be as blunt as my dear daddy's pocketknife. I thought your name was someone's idea of a joke, myself." The two siblings shared a nod of agreement. "What with your recent trouble with the law and all."

The Berdize siblings shared the same oval-shaped face, ash brown with pink highlights pixie cut, and a single dimple in the right cheek. According to Jane's research, they also owned and operated the dating service in use today. Over the years, it had become a regular part of their event planning empire. Along with the dating service, the sisters handled weddings, anniversaries, and various fundraisers throughout the year. Though three years apart, the pair did everything together while maintaining a fierce rivalry.

"Jane," Fiona prompted again.

Right. The sisters had questioned her appearance. "I don't have any problems with the law." The law had problems with *Jane.* She tugged *Truth Be Told* from her purse, the receipt she'd printed tucked inside. "Paid in full."

Audrey crossed her arms, the *Dr. Love* T-shirt stretching taut across her ample chest. "No offense, but are you sure you want to be dating right now, sugar?"

Fiona draped her arm over Jane's shoulder. "Baby girl has done nothing wrong. She can't help it if people keep dumping bodies at her home."

For some reason, Beau made a grunting sound.

Jane forced a laugh, as if she had no cares. "Innocent until proven guilty, right?" Or guilty until proven innocent when you sounded high on thorn apple again.

Charlotte pulled a pencil from behind her ear, a lock of hair cupping her cheek. "Oh, let Jane participate. It isn't like she's some depraved serial killer. She's not even dating mere weeks after her husband's death!"

Wait, were they suggesting...? Jane fought a grin. That judgmental tone revealed more than the words. Yes, they were indeed discussing Tiffany Hotchkins—and they'd just offered a new lead for the case.

"Tiffany is dating someone new?" she asked, trying so, *so* hard to appear breezy. Yep. Definitely trying.

"She sure is." Audrey propped her hands on her hips as her sister withdrew the trio of tickets from the money box. "I guess you could say she met her fella at one of our events."

Jane accepted the outstretched tickets as Charlotte's expression brightened. The elder sister said, "I'll take the free advertising, but I'd rather have that wedding planning money!"

The siblings high-fived and bumped hips.

"Tell me more." Jane leaned forward as if she intended to lay down some juicy gossip of her own once she learned what she wanted. If the Berdize sisters enjoyed spilling tea, she would happily pass around the sugar. "Is the man worthy of her? She deserves someone great, probably."

Beau made another grunting sound, and Jane shot him a look. Seriously, the guy needed to put on a better front. Since she'd failed to find him the perfect lady, this was his chance to score someone on his own *and* solve a case. Win-win.

"Worthy?" Audrey snickered, then grabbed a thick black marker to write their names on sticker badges. "What I know is this. His name's Jake Stephenson. A town newbie, here for a fresh start. Everyone likes him, it seems. I mean, he scores more dates than the other guys, but they never seem to mind. He's a bit shy at times and prefers the one-on-one sessions. If I'm remembering correctly, he's a painter. Houses or portraits, I'm not sure. He's got a new lease on life, so he's finally ready to fall in love again. At least, that's what he told me when I grilled him—er, interviewed him to help find his best match."

A fresh start, huh? "Did he say why he needed that fresh start?" A bad breakup? A divorce? A felony?

"He and a longtime girlfriend split up," Audrey replied. "The gal broke his heart something fierce."

Hmm. The timing of his arrival was as questionable as the timing of the thorn apple. And why had he shared so much painful, personal information with strangers—gossipers, at that—just to get a date? Who did that? Better question: Did Jake grace Ana's list of suspects? Mr. Cheats. Crusty Crab. Sticky Fingers. The Black Widower. Lie Guy. Slick Willy. Governor Handsy. To name a few. And what about the three nicknames with stars? Art Amour, Dr. Sexy Evil and the Robber.

Wait. Art Amour. With this Jake guy being some kind of painter... Could it be as simple as that?

"Did Jake and Tiffany match right away?" Jane asked.

"Almost. He—" Audrey went quiet when her sister nudged her arm.

"We shouldn't discuss our other clients," Charlotte pointed out.

"But we should be rude and not answer direct questions? It's not like I'm violating a matchmaker code of ethics." Audrey rolled her eyes and propped her elbows on the table. "Anyway. We didn't actually...technically... set them up."

"Not that we'll be announcing that part in our advertising," Charlotte interjected, her qualms gone.

"It was so cute. Sometimes Jake couldn't hide how nervous he was around the ladies. While he went on a couple genuine dates, he avoided anything long term. Then Tiffany showed. She was having dinner with a friend. They struck up a conversation and boom. Instant connection. They've been hiding out at her house ever since, ignoring the rest of the world. Probably because they're embarrassed about the timing."

"Or because neighbors are super nosy?" Beau suggested.

"I bet you're right. Nosy neighbors are *the worst*." Audrey looked over her shoulder before leaning forward and saying softly, "You guys want to hear something weird?"

A thousand percent Jane did. Even Beau appeared interested.

"Did you know Tatiana Irons used to speed date here...while she was hooking up with Dr. Hotchkins? No doubt she used our events to cover up her dirty little secret." Audrey's eyes went wide. "Whoa, that came out wrong. We're sad that Tatiana died, of course. Super sad."

"Of course you are. As are we," Fiona piped up, fluttering a hand over her heart.

Jane was too busy reeling to respond. Ana had been one of Dr. Hotchkins's side slices? And Jane hadn't uncovered the information during her previous investigation? Uh...she might need to revise her opinion about her amazingly brilliant deductions. Although, the GBH hadn't pegged the journalist as a side slice either, so, really, there was no reason to revise anything. Her opinion stood: She rocked!

Fiona leaned in, ready to do her part and bleed these women of information. In a nice, kind way. "I heard Dr. Hots kept a sex pad for his favorite girls."

Truth or lie? If he *had* kept a sex hangout and Tiffany had found out, the widow might have erupted, enraged...

No. No, no, no. Jane absolutely would *not* blame the widow this time. Not without concrete proof. She'd made that mistake before, only to learn the innocent woman truly grieved the loss of her philandering husband.

"He sure enough did," Aubrey said with a firm nod. "From

what I heard, Tatiana was his *most* favorite. The one he planned to run away with. Poor Tatiana. Heartbroken and now dead." She eyed Jane with misgiving. "But who in their right mind would want to kill her? That's what has got my curiosity up."

There was that phrasing again. *Right mind.* And why were the Berdize sisters peering at her expectantly? Wait, did they await a confession from *Jane*? Or perhaps a list of her main suspects?

Amateurs. They clearly didn't understand how to run a covert investigation.

Why don't I show them how it's done? Jane narrowed her eyes, tilted her head and leaned closer, saying sternly, "I don't know. You tell me. Who *would* want to kill her?"

Audrey shrank back a little, as if unsettled, and shifted. "Well, I *have* heard *something.* I mean, it's just a whisper, but there's talk the killer has a hit list of the doctor's girlfriends and she—or he—plans to eliminate everyone on it."

"That must be a mighty long list," Fiona said.

The sisters echoed each other with almost identical laughs, saying in unison, "The longest."

"I've seen longer." Beau shrugged his broad shoulders. "Ana was one of only three favorites."

Hold up. Was he fishing for information with a baited hook, expertly herding the pair to tell him everything they knew? Or had he actually seen the list?

The sisters exploded in excitement. "Tell us everything! We've searched and searched the Headliner, but never managed to unearth the names."

Hmm. What if there *was* a killer targeting the lovers of Dr. Hots? This case might have nothing to do with Ana's myriad of investigations and everything to do with her own extracurricular activities.

And we're back to Tiffany Hotchkins. Just because the widow was innocent before didn't mean she was innocent now. Hurt and rage were a toxic combination, able to change a person. Enough to commit murder, though? And blame an innocent like Jane? Because yes, Tiffany had the same motive as Tony Miller. In fact, the two could have worked together. The ultimate payback for Ana and Jane.

Two birds, one thorn apple.

And what of Tiffany's new man? He'd done some speed dating and had probably met Ana. What had the journalist thought of him? Nicknamed him? And how soon could Jane arrange a meeting with the guy?

He was a newcomer to town...just like the last killer. Which either ruled him out or pointed the finger of guilt directly at him. For all she knew, Aurelian Hills attracted the murderously inclined. Honestly, what were the odds he'd moved to town mere weeks before a homicide occurred, and he was miraculously innocent? Pretty low in her book. Meaning, yes, this Jake Stephenson had just shot straight to the top of Jane's suspects list, right alongside Tiffany and Tony.

"—the Headliner," Beau was saying, pulling her from her musings. "It's there. That's all I'm saying on the matter," he added amid the sisters' protests.

Jane barely stopped herself from patting her friend on the back, so proud of him and his ability to weave mysteries. He kept everyone intrigued while offering nothing in return and —she sucked in a breath. Tony! He was in the ballroom. He'd just approached the bar, entering Jane's line of vision as he exchanged an empty glass for a full one.

Tony, the lawyer who'd seemed a little too determined to irritate Agent Hightower, to demand the police charge Jane or let her go, was a speed dater. He'd most likely known the victim, and he'd kept the information to himself.

No need to ponder his nickname. *Hello, Sir Drinks A Lot.*

Once again, Jane reeled, her thoughts whirling. What if the crime had nothing *and* everything to do with Ana's research? The killer could have two motives. The last one certainly had.

Tony is buried so deep in guilt, he'll need a shovel to get out.

The shovel! The key. Her heart leaped. As Fiona continued gossiping with Aubrey, gathering intel, Jane focused on Charlotte. "How do we earn a gold shovel key?"

"What are you even talking about?" Charlotte asked, her nose wrinkling with confusion.

She held up the paper ticket she'd printed. "I was led to believe we'd get a gold key in the shape of a shovel with the price of admission?"

"Girl, where in the world did you hear that? We give our clients a good time, but that's it. No free drinks either, so don't ask."

Had Ana gotten the engraved key from a dater? Jane nudged Beau, then nodded toward the guest list on the table and spoke from the side of her mouth. "Memorize the names."

She expected him to do some covert maneuvering to steal a couple peeks at the attendees. He simply reached out and snatched the clipboard.

When Charlotte complained, Beau smiled tightly and said, "If one of the other two names is on this list, I'll let you know. We don't want you or your guests in any danger, do we?"

"No. No, we don't." The other women all but melted. "Good thinking."

Okay, see? Now that's how you get things done, Beau!

He scanned every page in the stack. *Might as well seize this opportunity.* Jane withdrew her phone and stealthily snapped a picture of the names as she pretended to answer a text. Man, if the law ever caught a glimpse of her photo album…

Thankfully, they'd only gotten a warrant for the security feed, not her personal device.

Oh, look. Tony had indeed attended several events with Ana.

Jane ground her teeth. "Okay, Beau. We've used up enough of the kind ladies' time." She stored her phone and plucked the clipboard from his grip. She kissed Fiona's cheek, then left her behind to finish the information quest and nudged Beau around the table. They entered the dating hot zone.

"Have fun, hon," Fiona called. "I'll be in shortly."

As Jane and Beau stood in the doorway, she scanned the twenty or so other participants who'd already arrived. Her goal was simple: make nice with everyone and figure out who was who. Only forty-nine to go.

"Are you ready to get your flirt on and help keep me out of prison?" she asked Beau, smoothing the skirt of her polka dot dress.

"No." He offered no more.

She rolled her eyes. "Do it anyway."

Fiona sidled up to her other side and sighed, as if weary.

"Everything okay?" Jane asked her, immediately concerned. "I expected you to stay with them another five minutes. Minimum."

"Yeah, another dater stopped at the table and the Berdize fount of information dried up."

"Well, I for one am glad you're here. After witnessing Beau's lackluster performance with our hostesses, we need to give him a few go-to lines sure to impress the ladies. We don't want him to bomb this golden opportunity."

Her dearest friend brightened. "You're right."

Beau looked between them before pointing a finger at his chest. "*I'm* the one worrying you? Me?" He hiked his thumb at Jane. "When you've got Ms. Mistrust here? I'll have you know I've never gotten a complaint."

Fiona and Jane burst out laughing.

He frowned, and Jane sobered. "Oh," she said. "You're serious."

Fiona snatched his name tag from his grip and applied the sticker to his chest, telling him, "Look a woman in the eye the entire time she's talking to you. Except don't stare. That's rude."

He blinked at her. Slowly.

"If the conversation is rolling, go with the flow," Jane added. "But don't allow the flow to move too fast. Or too slow. That's boring."

A groan left him as he scrubbed a hand over his face.

"Are you listening, young man? We're giving you gold!" Fiona wagged a finger at him. "Whatever you do, stick to tried-and-true topics exclusively. They encourage comfortability. But also pepper in unexpected observations to jazz things up. Something sure to dazzle."

When he opened his mouth to respond with a refusal—judging by his darkening expression—Jane hurried to cut him off. "Do your best to make her laugh but keep the jokes to a minimum. Tell one too many, and she won't be laughing with you. She'll be laughing *at* you."

Rocking back on his flip-flops, he peered up at the ceiling. Praying internally for divine assistance?

Fiona piped up, "Most important part of all, it's not about what you say or don't say. It's about how you say it. Or don't say it. Remember that. Oh, and be casual but professional. Approachable but aloof. Be yourself, as if you were someone else." She ended her advice with a friendly pat to his arm. "You'll do just fine."

I couldn't have said it better myself.

"I don't even know what any of that means," Beau told

them with a grimace. He scanned the sea of dating hopefuls, and that grimace worsened. "Jail wouldn't be *too* bad for you, would it, Jane?"

"Hey, you tampered with evidence, buddy." She patted his shoulder. "You'll be in a cell next to mine."

Another scan of the dating hopefuls. A full body shudder. "I think I'm fine with jail. Let's turn ourselves in."

Laughing, she urged him forward. "Don't worry. I doubt the singles of Aurelian Hills will bite...too hard."

CHAPTER FIVE

"Five minutes to love!"
Heart Lake, Pennsylvania - Fast and Flirty Festival
5 Matches Made!

"What's the weirdest thing you've ever done with a dead body?" Jane's current "date" asked as he reached across the table to brush his fingertips over her knuckles.

Big nope! She shuddered and eased back—again. This wasn't the first, second or third time he'd reached across the table to caress some part of her. How she wished she'd worn a hat tonight. Hats conveyed a message. They said: *I am removed from this situation.* Subtitle: *Do not touch.*

The guy's name was Billy. He was Jane's age and a mechanic. He was also handsome in a picture-perfect kind of way. No doubt he'd spent hours styling his hair and curating his look, posing for photos before arriving.

She'd pegged him as Ana's Slick Willy. The only plus to this minus. Jane hoped Fiona and Beau were having better luck with their "dates."

"I bet you've done bad, bad things," Billy said with a leer. Dim lighting and flickering candles gave him a sinister air.

This five-minute session had lasted an eternity.

As soon as the timer dinged, the women were supposed to pick up their drinks and fork, discard their plate, if they'd selected something to eat, and move to the next get-to-know-you session. The men would remain at the small round tables covered with cloths of dusty rose and an array of desserts for the women to choose from. A sweet treat in case the date proved sour? Like a consolation prize. Beau occupied the center table. The Berdize sisters must have stationed him there on purpose. The eye candy of the event despite his atrocious attire. Someone each woman could look forward to meeting. Smart.

His assigned seating also gave Jane a bird's-eye view of his performance, which was sadly lacking, if she were being honest. Every time she'd peeked at him, he'd been as still as a statue, with his arms crossed over his chest. Now he simply peered at the poor girl opposite him, silent, as if daring her to complain. *Say something, man.*

"Dude!" Billy threw back his head and cackled, reminding her of his presence. "If you have to think this long and hard, you must have done some pretty gnarly stuff. Gotta admit. I'm even more intrigued."

Oops. Here she sat, mentally chastising Beau, forgetting about her own "date." What were they discussing, anyway? Oh, yes. Dead bodies. Doing her best to appear nonchalant, she asked, "Who wants to discuss their work? I'd rather hear about your hobbies. For example, I can often be found in my garden. Do *you* like to garden, Billy?" Did he grow his own thorn apple?

"If I'm not in my garage, fixing my bike, I'm riding it." He wiggled his brows. "The wilder the ride, the better."

Smile. For the case. She forced the corners of her lips to lift and attempted to bat her lashes. Something Jane had seen in movies. "Tell me about your romantic history." *Smooth, Jay Bird.* "Do you prefer brunettes or blondes?" Or strawberry blondes? "Do you seek something long term?"

Billy winced. "Can I be honest with you, June?"

Ugh. June was her half-sister. "Jane," she corrected. She wore a tag for crying out loud. "And I really wish you would."

"I like 'em breathing." He dropped his gaze to her chest. "I offer the best night of your life, and that's it."

Double ugh. Was this seriously the mate-pool women had to pick from?

Jane missed Conrad *so hard* right now. What was he doing? Who was he doing it with?

Uh-oh. Was that...no, surely not. But what if it *was* a stab of jealousy? Had the Ladling curse already struck? Even though she'd only fallen into like with him? Yep. Definitely only like. Had he already moved on from the two-time murder suspect? They hadn't spoken since Ana—

"Hey, are you okay?" Billy asked, now wide-eyed. He was staring at her hand...because she was gripping her fork.

Oops. Jane released the silverware and forced another smile. "Please, go on," she invited, "you were being honest with me."

He squirmed a bit, and she had to admit she enjoyed his fidgeting. But only a little. Not enough to feel guilty. "No one really expects forever anymore."

Had Ana searched for her forever, or just her big break?

Thanks to the curse, Jane herself didn't expect forever from anyone. Except, sometimes—occasionally—she thought she might, maybe, possibly wish to share something meaningful with... another person. No one specific, though. Not that it mattered.

Get this back on track. "Have you enjoyed many, um, fun

GENA SHOWALTER & JILL MONROE

nights with the other daters?" With Ana, perhaps? Maybe he'd tried something, and the journalist had rebuffed him, and he'd ended her life as a means of getting revenge.

A sheepish grin was his only response before the buzzer sounded. Oh, thank goodness! She had two minutes to move to the next assignment. She hopped to her feet, fork in hand as commanded by the hosts, and detoured to Beau's table, bending down, getting right in his face. "Why aren't you talking? You're just sitting there staring at the girls like some hot, dumb dummy."

He threw his hands up in the air. "I'm doing what you told me to do. Looking a woman in the eye when she's speaking."

Jane dragged in a deep, calming breath. "No woman is gonna spill her secrets with you glaring daggers at her. Just bring it down a notch, okay? Your goal is to look attentive but not too attentive. Really, Beau. At least *try*. For me."

Charlotte made a hurry motion at her from the sidelines.

Jane completed the journey to her next table, plopped into her seat, and dropped her silverware, done with it for the night. She couldn't trust herself not to use it as a weapon.

The man across from her glanced up to meet her gaze. "Hi." He stole a peek at her name tag. "Jane. I'm Gus. So. Um. Have you, um, attended many of these?"

He wrung his hands, as if uncomfortable. Why? She'd seen him earlier, before the event's official start. He'd used his smoky gray eyes and chiseled jaw to smoothly charm several ladies. So why be unnerved by the unintimidating Jane? Unless he suspected the reason for her presence—because he was somehow involved in the crime.

Okay, maybe she sometimes believed the worst of people. But in her defense, nearly everyone lived up to the expectation.

"This is my first time to speed date," Jane said. "My friend Tatiana recommended I come." Too obvious?

"Tatiana—oh, you mean Ana, right? Yeah. I remember her." He didn't miss a beat, going from too nervous back to too smooth. "The pretty redhead. She died, right?" His cheeks flushed bright red. "I mean, I'm sorry for your loss. She dated my friend—small world—and I liked her. Very sweet."

"Who's your friend?" She tried for a casual tone. She failed. "Maybe Ana mentioned him." In her notes.

"Oh. Uh. Robby Waynes. He met Ana here, actually."

Robby Waynes. Older brother of Abigail Waynes-Kirkland, another former suspect. Which meant the friend was legit—and he too, had a motive for pinning Ana's murder on Jane. Like the others, Jane had accused his sister of being involved in Dr. Hots's murder.

"Why did Robby quit coming? At least, I'm assuming he quit coming since he's not here." Time wasn't gonna get the better of her with this date. When you wanted forthright answers, you must ask forthright questions.

"Oh, uh." Gus got nervous again, shifting in his seat and pulling at his clothes. "Rob's still recovering from their breakup, I guess."

"Heartbreak is never fun." She rested her elbow on the table and chanced a glance Fiona's way. Her friend grinned from ear to ear as she spoke with a guy Jane's age. "Ana broke up with him, then?"

"I'm not sure how things went down."

Truth? Jane shifted her gaze in Beau's direction—the next "date" in her own lineup. Currently he hosted a lovely brunette who appeared as nervous as Gus sometimes did. And yet, Beau practically ignored the woman, giving her nothing but a nod as he typed on his cell phone.

Well. Taking instruction wasn't his strong suit. How

many times had Jane asked him to cash his paychecks for security work at the cemetery, and how many times had he done it? Zip. Zilch. Zero.

Beau's date bravely carried on, her voice rising in desperation. "I've always wanted to learn how to drive a stick."

Bringing out the big guns—cars. It worked; Beau perked up, glancing up from his screen. "Do it. You'll be glad you did if ever you're running for your life and need a getaway vehicle."

The woman licked her lips, not the least perturbed by his morbid response. "Maybe you can teach me sometime?"

"That isn't a service Peach State Security offers at this time," he said with a shrug.

Hopeless. Absolutely hopeless. No wonder he had no prospects. The poor guy needed Jane's help more than she'd ever realized.

"Jane?" Gus yanked her attention back to him.

Focus! "Tell me more about Robby's breakup. Hurry!" Mere seconds remained—

The bell sounded. Argh! The conversation had just edged in the right direction.

She made a mental note to visit Robby Waynes as soon as possible. "Let's continue this discussion after the event, all right?"

"Uh..." His gaze darted. "They had a fight, that's all I know. There's no need—"

"I agree. There's no need not to meet up after the event. See you then." Since he hadn't denied her invitation, she'd take that as a solid yes.

She moved on, plopping into the seat across from Beau, who immediately leaned into her.

"Don't you dare say this is ridiculous," she whisper-yelled at the same instant he hissed, "This is ridiculous!"

They leaned even closer to each other, so close their foreheads practically bumped. He glared at her, and she glared right back. His clean scent hit her, and it was much better than the thick layers of cologne she'd picked up from some of the others.

She canted her head toward the woman who'd just vacated the chair. "That girl basically asked you out on a date. A real one."

His eyes widened in surprise. He settled against the back of his seat and spread his arms, a satisfied smile suddenly teasing his lips. "I told you I had moves."

"Really? Because it seemed like you were tripping over everything she was putting down."

He pursed his lips. "I'm here to keep us both out of jail, not get a date."

"Why can't you do both?" she countered.

Sighing, he massaged his nape. "How about this? If you've learned anything of value by the end of the night, I will work for free for a month."

"You're already working for free." Imagine it. A chief security officer who labored for hours without a concern for his wages. It was a horror she had never expected to live. "I've slipped checks in your truck, but you've never even deposited them."

"Then I'll cash every single one of them if you've learned something of value as of this moment—that I don't already know."

Well, then... "Okay. Get this. There was a guy who used to come all the time, and he was super into Ana."

Beau lifted a brow. "Correct. His name is Robby Waynes, and he stopped coming to the events after he and Ana broke up."

"Yes, but did you know he's related—"

"To Abigail Waynes-Kirkland. Yes. Someone else you accused of murder."

"Two suspects for the price of one." She folded her arms against her chest. "It might not be new information to you, but it *is* new information."

"Robby is my hero right now, not a suspect. He ditched the speed dating. That kind of brilliance doesn't mess up or frame well-protected gravekeepers."

Don't smile. It will only encourage him. "Did you know Slick Willy is—"

"Billy the mechanic. Yes."

She shuddered. "How'd you figure that one out? I didn't clue in until the third illicit hand caress."

His nostrils flared. "The what now?" He narrowed his eyes in Billy's direction. "I'll take care of Slick Willy," he told her with a flat tone.

Realization came. "You think he's the most likely candidate for murder?" Had Beau forgotten Robby? And she hadn't even mentioned Gus.

The buzzer sounded.

Jane groaned, exasperated on every level. "Start flirting for information like a good partner. Fiona and I could use some help carrying the team, thank you very much," she grumbled at him, before moving on to the next.

Unfortunately, she learned next to nothing from the following two guys. Finally, though, she reached Tony. She hadn't changed her mind: He was Sir Drinks a Lot, guaranteed.

"Well, well. We meet again. How special." He reclined in his chair, all smug assurance. He'd rolled up the sleeves of his white button down and unfastened the collar. "Did Agent Ryan realize you were too much trouble to mess with?"

"Special Agent Ryan." Jane didn't bother playing her role with him. "And he thinks I'm just the right amount of trouble." Probably. Still? "By the way, you forgot to mention you'd met Ana."

He flushed and jolted upright. "I *knew* you'd bring that up, and I don't think I like your tone. Did I know her? Yes. Did I like and admire her? Not even a little." He drained his drink. "Did I murder her? No."

"Why keep your association with her quiet then?"

"Are you kidding? Because I wasn't looking forward to being accused of committing another murder." Several daters glanced in their direction with wide eyes and slack jaws, and Tony flushed. "Neither of which I committed," he added at a louder volume.

Exactly what a murderer would say! And exactly what she had said to Agent Hightower. But, in Jane's defense, she hadn't committed the crime.

"Let's say I believe in your innocence." She didn't, of course. He now occupied the number one slot, edging out Tiffany and Jake. Also, Jane was seriously considering firing him. But she probably wouldn't. His pennies on the dollar rate couldn't be beat. "Why would someone else kill Ana?"

His eyes bugged out. "You met her, right? Always snooping through everyone's business. Following people around town. Taking pictures. Secretly posting her crackpot theories on the Headliner."

"I'm still waiting to hear a reason for murder."

As he sputtered, Jane's thoughts clung to the Headliner. Ana had posted her theories? "How do you know she posted, if she posted in secret?"

"I saw her do it," he grated. "And before you ask, it's not my fault if I accidentally see a screen name over someone's shoulder. Which is EDTKTT, by the way."

A new lead! Jane almost bounced in her seat. Before she mixed up the letters, she swiped up her phone and texted the username to Fiona and Beau. "Why wouldn't you tell me this, either? Or the cops!"

"Like I really want anyone and everyone scouring the app,

pretending to be a detective and investigating every rumor, destroying other families," he said, his tone drier than Jane's first Thanksgiving turkey without Grandma Lily's aid.

Murmurs erupted around them, and Jane scanned the tables, curious. A movement at the corner of her eye drew her gaze left—she gasped. Conrad! Her heart rate went from zero to sixty. Well, not zero. She still lived. But if she'd been a corpse, she might have spontaneously resurrected. The special agent had just strolled inside and paused all casual like.

What was he doing here? And why did he have to look so delicious? He wore a dark suit and a blue tie, and an almost-smile. No earthly being could have assembled a more perfect man.

He moved deeper into the room. When he reached an empty table, he removed his jacket and rolled up his sleeves, just as Tony had done. Unlike Tony, he left her drooling. No man had better forearms than Conrad. Strong, with a light dusting of black hair, tattoos on full display. Stick figures, clouds, and awkward houses; images a little kid from his past might have drawn. A well-cared for Rolex rested against his wrist.

She'd never asked about the tattoos, but she'd wondered. Was the artwork created by someone he knew—or had known? If so, why wouldn't he just say? Would he make her ask? Did he *want* her to ask? He was so closed off when it came to his past. Although yes, okay. He *had* tried to talk to her about personal matters at the conclusion of the last case. He might have spilled all then. To be honest, he'd looked ready to spill. Why, why, why had she panicked and shut down the conversation?

His gaze zoomed to her and narrowed, and she jumped to her feet. There was no stopping the action. He seemed to steel himself for a blow before stuffing his hands in his pockets and closing the distance.

When he stood before her, he stopped and traced his gaze over her face. His expression revealed little. But gradually, his features softened, and she could breathe again.

Finally, he gifted her with a lopsided grin. "Have you found the man of your dreams yet, sweetheart?"

CHAPTER SIX

"Rotate a date!"
Happy Corner, New Hampshire - The Old and the Beautiful
Mingler
11 Matches Made

*F*orget fake dating for a case. Forget the case entirely. When Conrad drew her into his arms, Jane drew him into hers as well, thrilling. Oh, how she had missed this man. Nothing beat his strong, comforting embrace.

No, not true. His spicy scent infiltrated her senses. This. This beat everything. She might—might!—have gotten high again. Possibly higher. If he bottled this fragrance, he'd make billions.

"How did you find me?" she asked, a lump growing in her throat.

The look he gave her—*baby, please.* "Hunting people is

what I do." He offered her a there-and-gone smile. "Also, Beau texted me, keeping me updated."

He had? Without enlightening Jane? She didn't know if she should be irritated or delighted. "How can you associate with me tonight when you couldn't before?" Gasping, she raised her head to peer up at him. "Is my good name cleared?"

"I couldn't associate with you and remain on the case. I wanted a look at the evidence, so I decided to go with option two." He threaded fingers in the hair at her nape and rested his other hand on her lower back just as the buzzer sounded. As people got up and shuffled about, Conrad told her, "You are no longer a suspect... at the moment."

She rocked on her feet before steadying herself. "Well, of course I'm not! I'm innocent." She far preferred being the investigator than the investigatee. "But, um, what convinced Agent Hightower?"

"For starters, nothing concrete has come up against you. Everything is explainable. But Hightower does believe you're involved in some way, and she's gunning hard. She says you have—quote unquote—a darkness inside you."

Darkness? Jane? Did he agree?

"Since I'm not allowed to officially work the case and you are mostly absolved," he continued, "I decided to take personal leave. Something I was due. I've always volunteered for weekends and holiday shifts, and I've never vacationed. And, now that I'm no longer going into the office, I can spend as much time with you as I want."

A simple admission, but so much to unpack. Where did she even begin? The fact that he'd never taken time off before this? His lack of holiday cheer? His desire to be with her?

"Come on." He tugged on his jacket and repositioned her against him, wrapping an arm around her waist. "Let's get you home. You can show me everything you suspect and why, then tell me what you did to the body while the security camera supposedly shifted to Rolex. As if I wouldn't notice the curtains. We'll solve this one together. No," he said when she opened her mouth to respond. "Don't tell me to return to the office. You need all the help you can get. Hightower is known for her extremely high clearance rate, obsessive need to prove herself and lack of give."

Okay. He sounded so admiring of the woman's "lack of give." Which was a troubling development for Jane, considering she herself was all give. But even still, he was here, and that counted for something.

That counted for a whole lot, actually. By-the-book Conrad was willingly venturing off road, perhaps even against direct orders, to aid Cemetery Girl. Her heart thudded at the realization, and a smile bloomed. She beamed up at him, melting into his side. This guy was *so* into her.

Wait. This kind of romantic gesture might be a bad thing. Extremely bad. The more he did things like this, the more likely she was to fall in love with him, and Jane absolutely, positively refused to fall in love with him. The second she did, *boom!* They'd be over.

Trembling now, she straightened to increase the distance between them. Go home and be alone with him? Not smart right now. Nope. Not even a little. "We should stay here a little longer. After the event, I'm meeting with a guy for drinks. Gus something."

Conrad stiffened for some reason. Did he know something she didn't?

"He's friends with Robby Waynes," she continued, "so surely he'll have some information for us."

As Conrad relaxed, she spied Gus striding toward the door with his newest date hanging on his arm.

Wow. To make plans with one woman and leave with

another... Where was the honor? Conrad would never do something like that. Jane rested her head on his shoulder.

Red alert! Red alert! She shouldn't admire him like this. Her defenses might crumble.

Straightening again, she attempted to ease back a step. Conrad held on tight and even rolled his eyes.

"Wipe the panic off your face," he told her. "I accept your rules. We'll keep playing will-they-or-won't-they as long as you need. I'm right here, and I'm not going anywhere."

Part of her kind of wanted to pretend she didn't understand his meaning. The other part believed that was the sweetest thing anyone had ever said to her. Which made her panic lessen, but also a thousand times worse.

"Now," he continued. "Tell me about the guy *we* are having drinks with, and I'll tell you what I know about Robby Waynes."

He'd learned something already? "There's nothing for me to tell since Gus just left with someone else."

"Then tell me why you planned to speak with him, and why his friendship with Robby Waynes matters to you."

That hadn't been their deal, but she rolled with it. "Get this. Gus threw his supposed friend under the bus with an information tidal wave to me, a stranger. From everything he admitted, I'm guessing Robby fell for Ana. They went out on a handful of dates, then fought for some reason and broke up. But what if Gus loved her too? Or, what if–"

"I'll stop you there and tell you Mr. Waynes was spotted with Miss Irons the morning she died."

What! "He *totally* could have poisoned her coffee."

Conrad didn't respond to her statement. He offered one of his own, his tone growing low and suggestive. "I want to take you home. Say yes, and I'll let you interrogate *me*. There'll be no limit on the topic or number of questions. The case. My past. I'll even throw in a bonus and pretend your curiosity about me means nothing."

Um. That wasn't a deal she could pass up. "Fine. But only because you're so desperate to share." She preferred to go straight to the source, anyway, rather than meeting with the friend. Which meant, yes, she would have a face-to-face with Robby Waynes. Tomorrow. "I'm sure Rolex is eager to draw your blood."

He gave her a wry smile. "Perfect. I've been looking forward to receiving my next claw shaped scar."

After she'd gathered her things, he led her toward the door. She cast a glance at Fiona and got a hearty thumbs up. Beau nodded, his expression revealing nothing.

"Hold up, Jane," Tony Miller called, striding over. He focused on Conrad. "Where are you taking my client, agent?"

He may be cheap and compromised as heck, but Jane had to admire his go-to attitude.

"She's no longer a person of interest." Conrad slid his gaze to her and arched a brow. "You can fire him if you'd like."

Tony's jaw dropped. "I got her off the suspects list?" He slapped his thigh and smirked up at the ceiling, saying, "Can't win a case even if I nail the judge, Emma? Wrong again, baby girl." He turned his attention to Jane and grew serious once more. "I'll be sending you a bill."

"Don't forget to include my discount." Really, she should send *him* a bill. She'd basically gotten *herself* off that suspect list, improving his professional reputation.

"I won't. I won't forget our consultation tonight either," he said and hurried on before she could blast him with protests. Consultation? "I'm just glad Hightower saw things my way." He looked to Conrad, almost hopeful. "She didn't, uh, mention me, did she?"

"No," Conrad replied. "She didn't."

A line formed between Jane's brows. "Why would she?" Did he have a *crush* on the agent? Or was he up to something?

Tony bowed up as if she'd slapped him and spread his arms wide. "Why would she? Because she couldn't get enough of ole Tony Miller. She kept eating me up with her eyes. That's why." All growly and snarly, he pivoted and aimed for the bar.

"Jane, the innocent ego shredder," Conrad muttered, ushering her toward the exit.

They bypassed the greeting table where the Berdize sisters waited. "Hey, where are you going, Jane?" Charlotte asked as they approached. "You can't date him. He didn't purchase a ticket."

With his free hand, he opened one side of his suit jacket, flashing his badge. "I've placed Miss Ladling under citizen's arrest."

The siblings gaped, and Jane bit her tongue to silence a ridiculous giggle. No doubt the duo would live off this new bit of gossip for days.

Audrey slapped Charlotte's shoulder. "I told you we shouldn't welcome murder suspects."

"What'd she do?" Charlotte demanded of Conrad, leaning forward.

"She disturbed my peace."

Jane laughed as he maneuvered her through the inn's lobby and past the ornate wooden doors that were original to the estate. Outside, the sun was beginning to set, painting the darkening sky with streaks of pinks and golds.

What a great day this had turned out to be. *Leads and direction and romance, oh my.*

They reached the crowded parking lot; her vehicle wasn't difficult to identify. The only hearse in the vicinity. Conrad propelled her to the passenger side and attempted to claim the keys, but she kept them out of his reach and shook her head.

"My car. I drive. Where's your sedan, anyway?" Did he not get to use the company transportation while on vacation?

"I'll pick it up in the morning."

Her grip tightened on her purse. Did he plan to sleep at her house? He'd said he knew the rules, but did he really? New panic flared. Thanks to her, they hadn't discussed their maybe-maybe not relationship expectations yet. Meaning, he hadn't agreed to her non-negotiable terms: totally casual but utterly exclusive, with no mentions of love allowed. But, like almost everyone else, he probably needed those mentions.

Heck, he might be getting them from others on the daily. A queue of interested beauties probably formed at his front door every morning. And why wouldn't it? He was a wonderful man. Caring. Loyal. Smart. Jane was cagey at best. If she wasn't gonna lock down his affections, she couldn't complain when he shared them with others.

Her stomach churned—until Conrad gave his eyes another roll and said, "I'm staying with Beau tonight. He's picking me up at your house after he meets his true love this evening." His dry tone drew a chuckle from her. "Trust me, sweetheart. I meant what I told you. I'm not trying to rush this thing with you." He grew as serious as cholesterol clogged arteries as he rubbed a knuckle on the underside of her chin, making her shiver. "Some things are worth waiting for."

"Really?" she asked, then chewed on her bottom lip, feeling more vulnerable than ever before. How *long* were these certain things worth waiting for, exactly?

"I'll go as slow as you need, I swear it. We'll get this right."

Don't ask him why he's willing to do this. And don't you dare

NO GRAVESTONE LEFT UNTURNED

ponder the curse. The consequences of risking a relationship. The pain that came with a loss.

You're pondering. Stop!

Her heart fluttered. "Thank you, Conrad." After planting a swift kiss on his cheek, earning a proud smile from him, she jogged to the driver's side.

He settled into the passenger seat and within minutes, they were buckled up and sailing down the road. Since the Manor was so close to Tiffany Hotchkins's house—no more than a five-minute drive, ten max—why not take a detour? To return to the Garden of Memories, Jane needed to pass the gated community, anyway... if she made a wrong turn into the neighborhood. Which she did. A quick drive-by wouldn't hurt anything.

She stopped at a security gate...where she punched in the code. Everyone in town knew it. No big deal.

"What are you doing, Jane?" Conrad sounded resigned. "This isn't the way to the cemetery."

"We're taking the scenic route? Enjoying a leisurely drive together before getting down to business? Which excuse do you prefer?"

He groaned as she drove down Tiffany's street at a crawl. The three-story sprawling mansion loomed ahead, golden light filtering through picturesque windows. The widow must be home. With Jake?

"Just so you know, Mrs. Hotchkins isn't Ana's killer," Conrad announced.

"How can you be so sure?"

"I personally looked into everyone who could possibly hold a grudge against you, and her alibi checked out."

"And people can't hire killers to do the dirty work for them?" Or date one?

He snorted.

From the corner of her eye, she spotted a sleek black

sports car speeding down Tiffany's long, winding driveway. On accident—honest!—Jane slammed on her brakes, blocking the only exit.

The sports car screeched to a halt. Seconds later, the passenger door swung open and Tiffany emerged. The driver remained inside the vehicle. Jane squinted at the tinted windshield, but she could only make out the boxy shape of a man. *Hello, Jake.*

Illuminated by the car's headlights, a frowning Widow Hotchkins strode over. The driver side of Jane's hearse faced the other woman. She rolled down the window with a million cranks of her wrist. No automatic button for her. Cool, crisp night air filled the cabin.

"Jane? Is that you?" the sophisticated beauty asked, adjusting the single shoulder strap on a curve-fitting black mini-dress. "What are you doing here?" Exasperation and curiosity laced her tone. That curiosity was a good thing, right?

But Jane couldn't get over Tiffany's transformation. No more red-rimmed green eyes. Gone was the coifed, under-stated elegance she'd adopted as a doctor's wife. Wild hair, six-inch stilettos and a sexy outfit said one thing—*woman on the prowl*. Did the guy in the driver's seat hope to be her next meal?

"Jane?" Tiffany prompted. "You *are* here for a reason, aren't you?"

"Oh, um, yes. I'm driving with my boyfriend. Not that he's my boyfriend. He isn't even technically one of my fifteen dates tonight." Her cheeks heated. "I mean, he's obviously my date tonight because we're together. Not that we're *together* together. We're still figuring things out. We haven't put a label on it or anything but—" *Shut up. Just shut up.*

Conrad offered the brunette a courteous wave. "Hi. I'm the boyfriend."

"Yes, I remember you. The cop." Tiffany narrowed her eyes before returning her attention to Jane. "I'll ask again. What are you doing here?"

"I saw your car and my foot hit the brake. An automatic reflex, I bet. Anyone else would have experienced the same thing in my situation, I'm sure of it. Don't worry. The hearse isn't stuck. I can move it anytime."

Tiffany heaved a sigh. "It's no problem, really. Besides, I'm glad you're here."

Wait--*what?* "You are?"

"I've been meaning to reach out. I'm the one who owes you an apology." The widow gazed down at her wringing hands. "I treated you poorly after Marcus died. And I'd like to thank you for helping the authorities find out who hurt him." She glanced over her shoulder and waved the driver over. "What are you doing next Saturday evening? Why don't you come over? I'll make dinner. You can bring your boyfriend, and I'll bring mine."

Next Saturday night? An entire week from now. Dinner? Prepared by Tiffany and attended by Jake. An investigator's dream. Which struck Jane as suspicious. Why set themselves up for interrogation? Unless they hoped to interrogate *her*?

Stop that! Conrad was a super smart guy, and he considered Tiffany innocent. So, she just might be innocent. But she might also be guilty. That wasn't conjecture, but a fact. *Anyone* could be guilty. People did things. And what about this mysterious Jake? Why hadn't he gotten out of the car yet? Was he hiding?

"I...accept?" Jane said, glancing at Conrad.

The driver's side door of the sports car finally opened, and a handsome man with a mop of pale hair emerged. Golden tan. Square jaw. From here, she couldn't make out the color of his eyes.

He slid a cell phone into his pocket and strode closer with

an almost goofy smile. With his almost-loose but somehow too-tight T-shirt and beige slacks, he looked like he'd stepped out of an ad in *Beautiful People Magazine*.

Tiffany obviously had a type.

"My apologies," Jake said with an amused, indulgent tone. "My mother wouldn't let me hang up."

Tiffany beamed at him, and honestly, she'd never appeared happier. The guy seemed pretty ecstatic himself, beaming as he wrapped an arm around her waist, just as Conrad had done to Jane.

"Hello." The newcomer offered everyone an easy smile, as if he had nothing to hide. "Nice to meet you both."

Uh, why give off a nothing to hide vibe unless you were hiding something? Why come to Aurelian Hills for a fresh start? Why not a bigger town with more amenities for a painter?

"Guess what?" Tiffany gripped his arm. "Jane and Conrad are dining with us on Saturday."

"Wonderful." Jake scanned the vehicle, his cheerful mood devolving into confusion. "Do you mind if I ask why you're driving a hearse?"

The killer would have known the answer to that question —the very reason to ask it. "I own a local cemetery. The one where everyone likes to drop off their dead bodies." She watched his expression for any reaction to her words.

"That is kind of the point, isn't it?" He glanced at Tiffany for help. "Dead bodies belong in a cemetery."

The widow grinned and patted his chest. "I'll explain it later, baby."

Baby. A nickname for the guy already? Wow. Jane hadn't even given one to Conrad. Well, other than Agent Spice, but that didn't count because...just because.

A sudden laugh escaped Tiffany, as if Jake had tickled her; she jumped up and down. "Okay, I can't stand it anymore. Is it okay if I tell Jane our news? I have to tell *someone* or I'll burst." Without taking a breath or waiting for a response, she blurted out, "Jake is no longer my boyfriend." Radiating pure joy, she held up a hand and wiggled her fingers, revealing a huge diamond ring. "I'm the Future Mrs. Tiffany Stephenson!"

∼

TIFFANY. Engaged. First married, now engaged a second time, and Jane couldn't even keep a guy for more than a couple months, through no fault of her own. All blame belonged to the Ladling curse, and that was that. And it was so not fair!

She huffed out a breath. Okay, so maybe Fiona had been correct when she'd said Jane's expectation of a doomed end caused her to curse herself. But what if she took a risk, crashed, and burned, and became a shell of herself, never to enjoy happiness again? And she wasn't being dramatic right now. It could totally happen.

"That went well, huh?" she asked Conrad, steering the hearse through town, heading for the Garden.

"I'm interested in your definition of *well*," he replied. At least his dry tone contained no notes of anger. "I'd say things could have gone better."

Did he reference the dinner invitation or Jane's mortifying explanation about their relationship? Or both? "Has GBH looked into Tiffany's new fiancé?"

"There hasn't been a need to do so."

"Does that mean you guys had no idea she'd started dating again?"

He snorted. "No. That means there was no reason to do it. She was with him the morning of the murder."

"And he couldn't have snuck out?" Not only had Jake

moved to town right before Ana died, he'd met the journalist at Digging for Gold *and* he had a connection to Dr. Hots via the widow.

Conrad groaned. "I recognize that tone. Poor Jake just topped your list, didn't he?"

"Nope. He's been there for days. If it makes you feel any better, he shares the spot with several others."

She eased to a stop at the entrance to the cemetery, the hearse's brakes squeaking. The iron gate wasn't automatic—Grandma Lily had believed automatic anything removed an element of grace and elegance, so Jane had never installed one. Not that she could have afforded it. But. When she'd left this afternoon, she'd shut the gate behind her and locked up. Now it was open. Either someone had broken in, or Fiona and Beau had beaten her home, though they should still be at the inn, learning as much as possible about the other speed daters. Most likely the latter.

She eased up the drive, navigating the twists and turns with practiced precision. Colored solar lights lined the sides of the black tar road, aiding moonlight and headlights. Nothing seemed out of place. A gentle wind rustled tree limbs together, encouraging the branches to welcome her home with a round of applause.

The caretaker's cottage came into view, with its wraparound porch and blue shutters bracketing the windowpanes. Nostalgia filled her. Once, Grandma Lily would have been sitting on a rocker, waiting for her. Her chest tightened as she parked under a gigantic oak, between Beau's truck and Fiona's convertible. The two were already inside the house. Both had a key.

To be here already... They must have left the event mere minutes after Jane and Conrad. Was *anyone* taking this case seriously?

Conrad blew out a breath and raked a hand through his

dark hair. Several strands refused to fall and remained standing, sticking out in spikes. Even exasperated, he was gorgeous.

"Anything else you'd like to discuss with me before we go in?" he asked when she killed the engine and tossed the car keys into her purse. "Or shall we kick off your interrogation?"

"There are lots of things I'd like to discuss with you." In the sudden quiet and darkness, however, a twinge of jitters nearly got the better of her. Instead, she forged ahead. "But we'll start with the interrogation. Namely, I'm interested in Ana's stories." The journalist's accusations were never far from her mind.

"All right. The interrogation," he said. Disappointment edged his tone. Which left her disappointed in *herself*. "If even half of her accusations are correct, Aurelian Hills is basically a penal colony in the making. Neighborhood watches that facilitate thefts not safety. Counterfeit coupon rings. Secret society hazings. She also suspected the cemetery of being part of an underground gold smuggling operation."

"What!" Yes, Dr. Hot's killer had claimed to find a nugget on the property, but no other nuggets had been discovered since. And Jane had searched. A lot. "Ana was *so* not right about the cemetery."

"Yes. True." He unbuckled and reached over to link his fingers with hers. "Hightower is investigating the speed daters, but nothing nefarious has popped up."

"Yet," she corrected. Comfort accompanied contact as his rough palm pressed against hers.

"Yet," he agreed. "While I'm in town, I plan to chat with some people about a few of Ana's other stories. And no, you may not join me."

"Why would I want to join you on such a fruitless endeavor?" Other than longing to be by his side.

They sat in silence for a moment, his scent infusing her every breath...and maybe, possibly, fogging her head, threatening her inner most defenses.

"Jane," he said, his tone gentler.

Just as before, when he'd come over and tried to discuss their relationship, she panicked like some silly schoolgirl, and there was no stopping it. Her inhalations turned shallow. Uttering her deepest thoughts and feelings would solidify this...thing between them. There'd be no going back.

The sooner they started, the sooner they ended.

Not ready. She'd lost so many people already, in one way or another. First her parents. Then her grandparents. Both of her boyfriends. One day, she would lose Fiona and Rolex. They couldn't live forever. Jane would become a shell of herself. No way she would survive losing anyone else.

Hating herself, she returned the conversation to the case. "Has anyone mentioned Dr. Hotchkins's list of favorite girlfriends? It's supposedly floating around on the Headliner. Beau might have mentioned it since you guys love texting each other apparently."

Another pause. A weary sigh. "I've seen the list, yes."

She perked up. "The hosts of tonight's event believe the doctor's side slices are in danger."

"Doubtful. There are fifty-eight names in total. Thirty-six sure things and twenty-two possibilities. Ana put it together. She added a star next to three women. Caroline Whittington, Emma Miller and Abigail Waynes-Kirkland."

Caroline. Dr. Hots's murderer. Emma, Tony's ex. Abigail, Robby's sister. Interesting.

"Theories about Mrs. Waynes-Kirkland and her brother Mr. Waynes are prevalent in some of the notebooks we took from Ana's apartment. She believed the siblings recently acquired jobs at the museum to steal documents from the *Gold Fever!* exhibit and replace everything with forgeries. Hightower is doing a deep dive on them both before setting up meetings."

Knew there was a connection! Jane had planned to hunt down Robby tomorrow. A museum drop-by meant she'd get to speak with Abigail too.

"Now," Conrad said, shifting in his seat to face her fully and unveil a grim expression. He never loosened his grip on her hand. In fact, he held on tighter. "I'm rethinking my strategy with you. I think I made a mistake, not pushing you and your fear of the curse, at least a little. It keeps things murky and allows you to jump to conclusions. So. I'm switching approaches. Nothing major, though. All right? But I want you to feel free to push back. Or not. Your choice. You ready?"

"No!"

"Too bad. Here goes. You believe you're cursed. Despite the implications of this, I like you. Romantically. I want to date you."

"Casually but also exclusively?" she managed to squeak out. "Even knowing we're doomed?"

"Yes and yes. Though I don't believe the doomed part." He waited a moment. "Will you tell me more about the curse?"

Though she trembled with surprise, excitement, and dread—he wanted what she wanted!—she nodded. She owed him that much. "It's generational and affects only the women of the family. None of us have ever kept the man we love."

"So you believe we'll split up as soon as we fall in love?" His gentle tone helped fortify her resolve to continue.

"Not as soon as, no. Sometimes a few weeks, months or even years pass before the inevitable end." Pops and Grandma Lily had lasted over a decade.

He tilted his head to the side, deepening his study of her.

Shadows crouched his features. "What about your mother? She's been married for almost twenty years."

"Only because she settled for a guy she doesn't really like."

"And there's no way to break the cycle?"

"None. The Ladlings have tried, trust me." Her grand-mother had always sworn her love for her husband sent him to an early grave. A guilt Jane never wished to carry.

Conrad stroked his jaw. "How about this? Every time we're together, I promise to do my best to give you a reason not to fall for me." He reached over and hooked a lock of hair behind her ear. "I rarely put my dirty clothes inside the hamper. They usually end up piled on the floor."

"The horror," she gasped out with a mock shudder, certain her eyes were sparkling with mirth. "But you should go on. This is working."

He snorted. "You are such a brat."

She heard his affection in every syllable and her panic returned and redoubled, punching her dead center in the chest. Breathing was suddenly a luxury of the past. Rather than run this time, she gathered her courage and asked, "Why do you like me? Why are you willing to go to so much trouble for me?"

He blinked at her, as if she'd just presented an unsolvable puzzle. "It would be easier to tell you what I don't like. Namely, your resistance to my charms," he added with a teasing wink. "Also your propensity to rush headlong into danger. And your avoidance of certain topics." He paused to arch a brow. "What do you feel for me? What do you want from me?"

Tremors racked her. "I-I like you too, despite your habit of accusing me of murder, and I don't want either of us to see anyone else. Even though we aren't official." Okay. Enough sharing for one day. She extracted from his touch and unbuckled, saying, "Is that Fiona in the doorway, waving us inside?"

The corners of his mouth quirked. "No one is standing in the doorway, Jane. But honestly, you lasted a whole lot longer than I thought you would. Admitted more, too."

No time to respond. She'd already flung open the door and entered the warmth of the night. Conrad wasn't far behind. He met her in front of the hearse and settled a hand on the small of her back. His heat seeped past her dress, caressing her skin.

"Don't worry," he said. "I'm done pushing tonight. I'll continue to give you space until you're ready for more."

Her tremors gradually faded. But, dang it, he'd used a super gentle tone, making tears sting her eyes. The knob on the screen rattled, interrupting their discussion, saving Jane from having to cobble together a response.

Fiona appeared, pushing open the screen door and holding out a small box before Jane could make a grab for the handle. "This was delivered while we were out."

Ana's coffee!

Conrad must have read the label and made the connection because he groaned and said, "You did not."

"Well." She rocked from the balls of her feet to her heels.

"Where have you been, anyway?" her amazing friend demanded, saving her from having to say anything more. "We've already gone through half of Ana's posts on the Headliner. Wait till you see who she blamed for what!"

CHAPTER SEVEN

"Rapid review in the queue!"
Darling, Minnesota - Find Your Mine Affair
8 Matches Made

ind officially blown. Jane remained staggered as she and the other members of Team Truth perched at her long, rectangular table in the dining room, with papers scattered about. Behind them was a chipped yellow laminate countertop and two barrel-back wooden chairs that separated the space from the kitchen.

They dissected every post Ana had made on the Headliner via her secret identity. Things Ana hadn't mentioned in her other notes. Not the ones Jane had photographed, at least.

Apparently, Aurelian Hills might have an arsonist skulking the neighborhoods.

Someone might have attempted to poison the entire congregation of First Community Church with a meatloaf casserole at a Sunday potluck.

A cheese smuggling ring used the old mine lights to signal each other.

Holt's Bakery covertly housed an underground casino in the basement.

Best of all, Jane identified more than half of the sixteen speed daters with nicknames. EDTKTT never held back her slanderous accusations. She'd directed much of her malice at The Robber, someone who had stolen cash and other things from a plethora of daters (allegedly).

Robber. Robby. Coincidence? Jane thought not.

Conrad, Beau, and Fiona stayed at the cottage until well past midnight, everyone relaxed in the kitchen, chomping on a platter of chicken nachos with homemade cheese sauce as they pored over every word from their phones and laptops. Sometimes someone read snippets aloud for the rest of the group. Jane even dared to share her personal portfolio of crime scene photos with her…boyfriend.

Maybe if she repeatedly said the word, it'd be easier to accept. Boyfriend, boyfriend, boyfriend.

Her…boyfriend looked from the photos to her face again and again. Nope, not easier. "Do I want to know how you photographed the contents of a dead woman's purse?" He glanced over toward Beau. "The zoom on Rolex was a nice touch, by the way," he muttered. "I *will* be viewing the footage in its entirety before I leave tonight."

"I don't think that's wise," Jane began. She didn't want to get Beau in trouble.

"Tough. It's happening."

She heaved a sigh. "Fine."

Beau shook his head, as if saddened. "You are the worst criminal."

"Are you saying I'm as bad at committing crime as you are at flirting?" Jane asked with her snottiest tone, earning a snicker from Fiona. "If so, I think I might be offended."

Amusement sparkled in his eyes. "Moving on. I think we can all agree the Waynes siblings should be questioned."

"Which Hightower will do," Conrad piped up. "I think we can also agree Jane shouldn't do any of the questioning."

"I believe she should." Fiona gave him a pitying look. "Considering she and I are co-captains of our team, you boys are overruled."

Jane blew her best friend in all the world a kiss, then ruined the gesture with a jaw-cracking yawn. Oh, wow. Fatigue was catching up with her.

"All right, time for us to go," Conrad said, standing.

Everyone helped her clean up and left shortly thereafter; her agent was the last one through the front door, however. He cast her a lingering glance and brushed his fingers against her hand.

"I'm the world's worst cook," he told her. "I'll prepare you a meal one day and you'll never again worry about falling in love with me."

"You'd think. But an apron probably makes your muscles pop. How am I supposed to resist you then?"

His lopsided grin was in place as he headed for Beau's truck. Jane sighed soulfully. Mournfully. Dreamily.

That night, she snuggled Rolex, as usual, but for once, she couldn't sleep. Her mind stayed busy. Every time she thought of Conrad, which was often, she forced herself to switch tracks and make plans. Plans she executed the next morning, after preparing a cup of Ana's coffee.

The cold brew specialty blend needed to steep for an extended period, like tea. So, Jane let it steep in a large travel mug as she drove to the Gold Rush Museum. Her second trip to the place in less than two months. Conrad and Beau would protest as soon as they found out, but so what? They were too intimidating to pull this off. Who would open up to them? And also, Jane kind of looked forward to rubbing their noses in her success. But only kind of, so it was okay.

A blast of cool air ruffled her bangs and the brim of her hat as she stepped through the heavy oak doors of the Gold Rush Museum, escaping glaring sunlight and intense heat. Once a courthouse built to impress, now home to the town's most beloved artifacts. Each year, guides enticed school children to examine the red brick walls for the specks of gold rumored to embed the clay.

She paid for entry, disappointed that neither Abigail nor Robby staffed the counter. During her last visit, she'd noticed a help desk nestled amongst the displays inside. Maybe she'd have better luck there.

Jane made her way down the now familiar portrait covered hallway. The click-clack of her low heels announced her presence, drawing the gaze of other patrons. A mother gathered her two children close, keeping an arm slung over each, as if protecting her cubs from a vicious beast. An older couple drew closer together and whispered.

Oookay. So. Rumors that Cemetery Girl might be involved in another murder had clearly spread.

Jane hardly cared. Truly. Her chest grew tight for a different reason; she just didn't know what it was.

As she passed the *Gold Fever!* exhibit, she wondered if Ana had been right. Had Abigail stolen and replaced certain documents? Specifically, the documents Jane had donated. Journal entries from her ancestor's days in the Order of Seven, a secret society of gold worshippers. Checking out the display would be her next task.

The Waynes siblings first. With four strikes against her, Abigail had sailed straight to the top. (1) Suspected side slice for Dr. Hots. (2) On the hunt for the cemetery's supposed cache of gold. (3) Disdain for Jane. And (4) Her brother's connection to speed dating and Ana herself.

Maybe Abigail had acted alone. Maybe her brother had helped her or even led the entire operation.

Maybe the pair were innocent...but probably not.

Jane spotted the help desk, the round stand covered in peach drawings made by schoolchildren. A colorful mural of men mining gold decorated the wall behind it. Oh! Robby staffed the counter.

Jane hurried her pace. He sat alone, perched in front of a computer, his attention focused on the screen. Same thick dark hair she vaguely remembered from their days at school.

She smoothed the sides of her purple dress and cleared her throat. "Hi, Robby!" She winced at her exuberance, but quickly slapped on a smile, stretching her neck to angle her hat and block out the rest of the world.

His dark head jerked up at her greeting. He blanched when he spotted her, his brown eyes slitting in recognition. Then he hurried to hide his telling reaction with a polite mask. "Hello and welcome to the Gold Rush Museum, where you don't have to dig to find a treasure. How may I help you?"

They'd never really spoken before. While they'd attended high school together, he'd been two grades younger and as popular as his sister. Jane's best friend had been the school janitor, Mr. Harvey.

"Where's Abigail?" she asked, adding a brighter shine to her smile, all *you can trust me, I'm as sweet as sugar.*

"Off today," he said, cautious now. "Why?"

What a disappointment. Might as well proceed with a bang. "Abigail helped me out after Dr. Hotchkins's death, and I'd like to return the favor." Truth. Sort of. Abigail had dropped the first clue: Dr. Hots and his infamous exam room vitamin D injections. Her words, not Jane's. "I came to tell her there are terrible rumors floating around. She's mentioned...and so are you."

"Me?" His hand shook as he reached for a can of soda he'd hidden behind a wall of sticky notes. Gulp, gulp, gulp. "What are people saying?" The question grated from him, as if he'd tried to hold it back.

Hmm. Interesting reaction. He was unwillingly intrigued.

Get into character. Jane looked left, right, then left again, really selling her need for secrecy, then leaned over the laminate counter. "Someone accused you two of murdering Tatiana Irons." *It was me.* No reason to mention the journals yet.

He flew to his feet, soda splashing over his hand, the chair wheeling back. Color drained from his face. "I didn't! Abby didn't either." His voice boomed, everyone nearby glancing over. An older employee put a finger to her lips to shush him. Robby scrambled for a wad of paper towels under the desk and blotted up the liquid he'd spilled. "I hated Ana, but I never hurt her. I wouldn't."

"Why did you hate her? You were dating, right? Gus says you guys had a fight or something."

A scowl drew his brows closer together as he tossed the damp towels in a trash can. "Gus has a big mouth."

Yes, he did. A nervous habit or redirecting guilt for some reason?

"Ana drained my accounts," Robby snapped. "Took every cent I had. Why do you think I'm working a second job here?"

Wait. "Ana stole from you?" The hard-hitting journalist?

"I swear on my life she did. I discovered the theft only a week before she died." He plopped into his chair and leaned back, as if the weight of the world had just settled on his shoulders. "I confronted her, and she blamed some guy. Said he was framing her for the theft of my savings to force her off his trail. But I knew better. On our dates, Ana constantly asked personal questions. Information she must have used to log in to my accounts."

Jane's every instinct pinged. There was something here. There must be. The Robber...a speed dating thief. That was no coincidence. But did this mean Robby *wasn't* The Robber? "Did she happen to mention the guy's name?"

"Yeah. Blake Crawford. Some real estate agent in Atlanta. Yes, I dug into his life online." He glared at her, as if she were responsible for his current predicament. "I haven't spoken to him, though. I haven't spoken to anyone."

A real estate agent might know his way around an illicit flower bed. And what if Ana *had* stolen from Robby, her stories nothing but wild speculation? What if she'd ripped off this Blake guy too, planning to pit one victim against the other? If Blake had any ties to speed dating or even Tiffany and Jake...

Hmm. Blake. Jake. Could rhyming names mean anything?

A mystery for later. If Blake had swindled Robby and framed Ana? What then?

Either way, Jane had just lined up her next person of interest. "You haven't spoken to anyone but the authorities, right?"

"Are you kidding?" Robby ran a hand through his hair. "One week I'm accusing Ana of theft, the next she's dead. I don't want to draw any unwanted attention to myself. Unless and until the cops visit me, I say nothing."

Uh... "Why tell me then?"

Robby laughed without humor. "You're the cemetery girl who helped GBH close the last case. So do us both a favor and help them close this one. And if not, well, this will all blow up in *your* face, not mine. That might be the best outcome for everyone."

Jane disliked him on the spot, but she also appreciated his

reasoning. That wouldn't stop her from busting him if he committed this crime. "Thanks for your help."

"Don't bother me again," he muttered.

"Okay. See you soon." She smiled brightly and waved. Time to check the display documents.

~

JANE NAVIGATED the streets of Aurelian Hills, heading home. Her hat rested in the passenger seat, and she sipped the iced coffee. Extremely bitter, almost undrinkable. No wonder Ana hadn't known her beverage had been laced.

Between drinks, Jane sang along to golden oldies that cranked from a playlist of her Pops's favorite songs. At each stoplight, she reflected on her next tasks. As soon as she had access to her computer and the journalist's notes, she planned to:

*Compare the photos she'd taken of the *Gold Fever!* exhibit with the photos of her donated items.

*Learn everything she could about Blake Crawford, the real estate agent, and Jake Stephenson. (Blake, Jake. Jake, Blake. *Was* there something there?)

*Crosscheck everything she learned about the pair with the sixteen daters as well as the list of Dr. Hots's serial bangs.

Interspersed with all of that, she anticipated cuddles with Rolex. Later, she intended to have dinner at the cottage with Conrad, who was staying at Beau's another night. Although… maybe Conrad would come over early and help her. With the tasks, not the cuddles. He *was* her boyfriend, so being at her beck and call was kind of part of the deal.

And okay, yes. That usage of boyfriend hadn't been as difficult as the others. Having a significant other didn't have to be scary. She would guard her heart. People dated without falling in love all the time. Anyway.

Filled with renewed hope, Jane turned into the cemetery's driveway. Oh, wow. Um. What was happening to her heartbeat? Because dang. The organ banged in her chest. Raced. Thudded. Sweat beaded on her brow and her upper lip. She panted her breaths. Was she dying? Tripping on more thorn apple? No, the only thing she'd ingested was...the coffee!

This was how Ana had lived on the daily?

Despite being a short distance from home, her most comfortable PJs, and her precious fur-child, Jane felt as if she were coming out of her skin. So jittery, in fact, she'd be calling Conrad and demanding he come over to calm her the heck down.

At the halfway point in the driveway, sunlight glinted off a piece of metal, and her mind screamed, *Wrong!* As wrong as her body. She knew this land forward, backward, up, down, and inside out. There should be no metal in this section. A loud squeak rang out as she slammed on the brakes with more force than necessary. Perfect timing. A guy streaked with dirt, glistening with sweat and holding a shovel stepped from behind a large, purple-flowered hydrangea bush.

He froze as she rolled down her window to shout at him. The crank usually required great effort on her part. Not today. Somehow, the coffee had given her superhuman strength.

Mr. Shovel lurched into a mad sprint. Off to the side waited a sedan, clogging the narrow drive threading through Autumn Grove.

The front of the vehicle faced her, granting her a good look at the driver. Abigail Waynes-Kirkland leaned over to open the passenger door, allowing Landon Kirkland, her on-again, off-again husband—Mr. Shovel himself—to dive inside. Tires peeled out, smoke rising as the car shot past hers.

Fury rose white-hot and blistering. A fury Jane had never

experienced before. Two people had dared to enter her property in broad daylight to dig up a grave and search for gold. Something they would only do if they'd spotted her leaving the grounds—and verified her chief security officer was on a break.

Operating solely on emotion, caffeine, and the heat of a thousand suns, Jane put the hearse in reverse, turned around as swiftly as possible, and gave chase. They thought they'd get away with this? *Think again.*

Pedal to the metal, she followed the sedan onto the main road. Air gusted through the open window, dancing locks of hair before her face. Her hat flew out, sucked from the seat.

The sedan snaked around a corner, and Jane followed, tires squealing. Had Robby known what his sister planned? Maybe not; he hadn't attempted to keep Jane close. On the other hand, he could have called the couple and warned them of her return. If Jane had arrived just a few minutes later...

She banged a fist against her steering wheel. Should she call Conrad? He was spending the day with Beau—Beau! He had access to the security cameras. What if Abigail and Landon had entered the house before wandering the grounds, scaring Rolex? Or worse!

Panic replaced fury. As she flew down the street, Jane frantically pressed the screen in her console. Beau had installed it as a surprise when he'd removed the old AM radio. Another task he'd refused to accept payment for.

He answered after two rings. "Hey, what's up? What's that noise?"

She screamed over the roar of wind, the words leaving her in a rushing, endless stream. "Where are you and will you please stop whatever you're doing immediately and tell me if someone entered the cottage and did something unspeakable to Rolex before they dug up a body or I will do murder for real?!"

Rasping breaths preceded the click-clack of a keyboard. In the background, Conrad demanded, "Is something wrong?"

"She's fine—kind of," Beau told the agent. "Rolex is fine too, Jane. He's sitting at the living room window, guarding the porch. And no one dug up anything. The cameras aren't showing any holes."

Okay. All right. No murder. Maybe. "I am steaming again. Absolutely steaming! By the way, I might be dying of a coffee induced heart attack."

With a commanding tone, he told her, "Take a deep breath and tell me what happened."

"Oh, I'll tell you, all right. It was Abigail and Landon." Jane flew along the town streets, faster and faster, yet her target still managed to get lost amid the other cars. Argh! She wove in and out of traffic, the wind kicking up. Dirt thickened the air.

"Jane. Continue."

"He was wandering the cemetery with a shovel, Beau. A shovel. As if the families of the dearly departed haven't been traumatized enough. Abigail is the getaway driver, but not a very good one." Jane punched at her horn.

"You are chasing them in the hearse?" Beau bellowed. "After drinking Ana's coffee?"

"She's what?" Conrad roared.

"Was I supposed to let the digging monsters escape?" she snapped.

Conrad must have snatched the phone from Beau, because he barked, "Pull over this second or I swear I'll—"

"I'm hanging up now," Jane said as she clicked the proper button, because hanging up without notice was rude.

Only a couple seconds later, her phone rang. Caller ID revealed Conrad's number. If she answered, he would only order her to back down again, not yet understanding that a *real* potential boyfriend would help her destroy her enemies, not encourage her to show mercy. And the Kirklands *were* her enemies. If they hadn't dug up a body, they'd planted evidence. Guaranteed. They must have killed Ana and thought to frame Jane to get her out of the way.

This was a declaration of war.

A new call came in. Conrad again. *Persistent agent.*

Jane refused to answer this time too. Now wasn't the time to explain the ins and outs to Dating 101. When she caught up to Abigail and Landon, she would... she...Argh! She was too furious to decide. Nothing sounded violent enough. But, as she honked her horn again, swerving to avoid an oncoming car, her heartbeat began to slow. She yawned, growing very tired, very fast.

Coming down from her caffeine high? She reached for the cup only to pause, rational thought intruding. A car chase in public, without backup? Seriously? Who did that? Especially when the chaser knew where the chasees lived.

What if she'd harmed a stray animal? Like, say, one of Rolex's relatives? Her fury deflated—no, not true. It redirected, focusing solely on herself, and she eased her foot from the pedal.

A siren blasted behind her as she eased into her next turn. She glanced at the rearview mirror. Red and blue lights flashed. Had the boys phoned the sheriff? Good thinking. No doubt the man needed to get her statement before arresting the Waynes. Maybe he'd even let her tag along and watch. She yawned again. Maybe he'd call her and tell her all about it.

Jane flipped her blinker, slowed, and parked on the side of the road. The wind died, and she looked around. Prospect Street. The Prospect Lodge B&B sat to her right, the outdoor coffee bar brimming with curious guests.

The sheriff parked behind her, emerged from his vehicle,

and approached. Sunlight glinted off his sweat-glistened head. His full silver beard, broad shoulders and barrel chest usually brought nothing but comfort. He was a good man who'd always taken care of the citizens he protected. Today, she only wished to shake him.

She leaned out, saying, "Here's what happened."

"Let me stop you there, because I don't care." At her side, he crossed his arms over his white button-up. Sunglasses shielded his eyes. He chewed on a toothpick. "You put innocent lives in danger, Jane."

"I know, and I'm so sorry! I promise it won't happen again. I'll never drink Ana's coffee either. Unless there's an emergency. Anyway. I'd just realized Rolex could have a parent or sibling roaming around out here. I'm not sure I could forgive myself if I'd hurt one of his family members."

She imagined hitting a bird, feathers flying everywhere. Hosting a dog or cat funeral for a gentle animal who'd only wanted a few hugs. Or having to face a mother raccoon who'd just lost her children, thanks to Jane's actions.

"That's not—never mind." The sheriff scoured a hand over his weary features. "If you'd hit another car, Jane. Someone could have died."

She shrank into her seat, the gravity of the situation suddenly hitting her full force. *Died.* The word echoed in her head. One syllable. Four letters. A thousand needles in her galloping heart. He was right. Her reckless actions could have led to a tragic end. Any of those people could have had a pet in their vehicle. Strays weren't the only fur-babies around.

Bile burned her throat. She'd let her outrage upset her level, rock steady sense.

"I'm going to put you in the back of my car and call your special agent to come get you," he continued in that same easy tone.

Guilt continued to well. "Is that what you'd normally do?" she asked, her throat thickening.

He rocked back on his heels. "No. I'd haul you in for reckless endangerment."

Her fingers tightened around the steering wheel, her nails digging into the unforgiving steel. She dragged in a breath, held it, then let it go slowly. "No, I can't let you give me special treatment. Guess I gotta learn this lesson the hard way." She loosened her death grip and shoved her hands through the open window, ready for him to cuff her wrists. "Uphold your sworn duty and take me to jail."

He scratched his thick white beard. "Now, hold on a minute. There's no reason to—"

"Don't you dare show me an ounce of leniency," she chided, already pushing her way out of the vehicle.

"Stop being dramatic, Jane."

She sputtered for a moment. "Caring about the animal kingdom is dramatic to you?" Wow. Just wow. "When did you lose your compassion, Sheriff?"

"You should care about people as much as animals."

"Now who's being dramatic? By the way, I help pay your salary, and I'm demanding you haul me to the clink this instant."

Pedestrians watched unabashedly from the sidelines— most of the people she was supposed to care about were filming the interaction from a safe distance with their cell phones.

No wonder she preferred animals. Still, she pressed her hands over her heart, calling, "Don't worry. Sheriff Moore is teaching me the terrible cost of participating in a high-speed chase."

"Jane—"

"I'm done arguing about this, Sheriff. You lock me in the slammer and throw away the key, or I'll be lodging a formal complaint with the city council. Then I'll come after your job! I'll find a way to become the next sheriff, just see if I don't."

"Lord save us all," he muttered. Heaving a sigh, he reached for his cuffs. "Jane Ladling, you have the right to remain silent..."

CHAPTER EIGHT

"Gotta start somewhere!"
Romeo, Michigan - Wherefore Art Thou Gala
77 Matches Made!

*T*he next morning, Jane paced the six feet length of her sterile jail cell until the bottom of her shoes no longer clacked. As the hours passed, more and more of the caffeine faded from her system, and more and more regret inundated her. Now she was certain she should spend the rest of her life rotting in here, surrounded by plain, gray brick and a stainless-steel toilet.

When she grew tired of pacing, she sat on the thin cot, alternating between stewing on her wrongdoing and lamenting her troubles. The Kirklands currently roamed free, and they clearly had an agenda.

Last night, she'd used her one and only phone call to rehire Tony via his voicemail. In her message, she instructed him to reach out to Conrad, Beau and Fiona. Fiona was to care for Rolex, and the boys were to inform Hightower about the Waynes's activities, search for any evidence they might have planted, and investigate Blake Crawford. Oh, and they were not to bail Jane out for any reason.

Had Tony done it, or had he failed her? He must have succeeded, considering no one had attempted to spring her.

While her sights remained on Abigail, Robby and Landon, she refused to rule out her attorney completely. For all she knew, he was aiding the threesome.

Had news of her arrest spread through town faster than peach butter on warm toast? Surely. So, what came next, legally speaking? On TV, people made a plea in front of the judge, followed by a dramatic bail pronouncement, ending with a climactic pounding of the gavel.

Jane had only one response planned: Guiltier than charged!

Fatigue wound its way through her limbs, and she curled into a ball. Everything was catching up to her. Worrying over Rolex's safety. Discovering no good, dirty evidence planters on her property. Thinking her home had been desecrated once again. Late nights studying Ana's notes. Tossing and turning, missing Conrad. A high-ish speed car chase. Losing her hat. The stress of not seeing the Kirklands in the cell next to hers.

Heavy footsteps caught her attention, and she sucked in a breath.

When the sheriff appeared, she jumped to her feet. "About time. You haven't even taken my fingerprints or mugshot yet."

He sighed. Keys jingled, and the bars creaked open. "You're free to go. Just do everyone a favor and drive safe."

"But—"

"Walk yourself out of the cell or I carry you. Your choice."

Jane humphed at him. "Just know I'm doing this under duress." Head high, she marched past him and stomped down the hall.

"Wrong way," he called.

Well. There went her perfect exit. She stomped back to his side.

His lips quirked the barest fraction as he pivoted and led her out of the three-story maze of offices, hallways, and stairs.

"Where's my car?" she asked. "Still on Prospect Street?"

"No, ma'am. Your friends took care of everything." He opened a door, revealing the first-floor lobby. "They all love you something fierce. I don't think I've ever been so subtly threatened with the loss of life and limb if I failed to release someone from my custody."

Her chest clenched, a wonderful and awful sensation. Somehow, she'd discovered some humans as good as animals, and she was lucky enough to call them her friends. She braced as she swept past him. Conrad jumped up from a stiff, uncushioned chair. His hair stuck out in spikes, and his five o'clock shadow lay thicker than usual along his strong jaw. His wrinkled white T-shirt might have coffee stains. Worry radiated from him, magnified by the lines of tension around his bloodshot eyes.

He looked *awful*, and her guilt surged anew. This man worked a high-stress job he managed to handle with detachment. And yet, Jane had worried him to incredible depths.

Would she do it again and again until he snapped, and the curse took effect?

The moisture in her mouth dried. *Barely a beginning, and I'm already planning the end.*

"I am so angry with you," he growled at her.

"I know. Just know you aren't as angry with me as I am with myself," she rasped, moving toward him. Walking...jogging... He opened his arms at the last moment, and she just kind of fell into him, wrapping herself around his big, powerful body. They clung to each other for a suspended minute, the only two people in existence.

She breathed deeply, inhaling the incredible spiciness of his scent. So good. Too good. The type of aroma a girl might miss when it was gone. "Where are the others?" she asked, her voice muffled against his shirt.

"They're at the cottage, awaiting your return. Come on, sweetheart," he said, already far calmer.

Oh, how she loved when he used that endearment. Her breath caught. Well, not loved. But liked, only liked.

He led her outside, and she let him, morning sunlight blistering her eyes and blurring her vision. Yes, sunlight not sadness at her doomed future.

Wow. Her hope must have withered in that jail cell.

"No more of Ana's coffee. Promise me." Conrad helped her into the passenger seat of his car.

"No more," she rasped, shuddering as she recalled its effects. "At least I can now report why Ana failed to notice the thorn apple. That cold brew is disgusting, and the caffeine must have dulled the initial effects as she drove to the gate." As she settled in, the comfort of it all zapped what remained of her strength. By the time her agent had settled behind the wheel, she had hooded eyelids and fought her latest yawn. At least she'd adjusted to the brightness, her eyesight clear.

He eased the car onto the main road, then reached over and claimed her hand, twining their fingers. Her insides squeezed. The best thing for them both? Solving this case. The sooner she cleared her name, the sooner everything could go back to normal. Whatever normal happened to be.

"Has anyone questioned the Kirklands for their actions on my property?" she asked. "They might have planted evidence to frame me for Ana's murder."

He groaned a little. "Jane. Come on. You know better. The

security footage shows that they did nothing wrong. They entered a public property to view the graves of their ancestors. There's no probable cause. So they carried a shovel? So what? They can say they found it on the grounds and moved it out of the way."

"Then we nail them for theft. If they found a shovel on the grounds, it's mine and I want it back. It's *invaluable* to me, so yes, I'm pressing charges."

"It's not your shovel. You have two and both are accounted for. I checked. Someone else could have left it. Or, the Kirklands can say they were digging up weeds on a loved one's plot."

"A lie! I *never* allow weeds to grow."

"They'll accuse you of terrorizing them for no reason."

Frustration ate at her, but still she said, "Fine. I get what you're saying. You believe with every fiber of your being that someone will make a blockbuster movie about Ana's death one day—the Curious Case of Cemetery Girl and Super Accuser—and *I'll* be cast as the villain." Honestly, that one stung a bit.

Although, it wouldn't be the *worst* movie ever made. A surprise hit, probably. Lots of people rooted for the bad guy nowadays.

"What kind of creature even are you?" Conrad asked with all kinds of awe. Yes. Awe.

She shrugged because she didn't know the answer. Perhaps time would tell. "Look. We both believe the Kirklands planted evidence against me or at least planned to open coffins to search for gold." She stretched as best she could, a yawn finally slipping free. "Maybe both."

"Maybe," Conrad said, surprising her by lifting their joined hands and kissing her knuckles. "But Beau and I launched a thorough search of the grounds yesterday. He hasn't stopped. That's why he's still at the cottage."

Both of her boys had dropped everything to help her... and not because they loved her. The sheriff was wrong about that. But, um, had the air gotten thicker? Breathing became more of a chore.

She focused on the conversation. "For the record, there's no need to tell me a terrible fact about yourself. I expected to languish in jail, paying my debt to society, never again endangering the local wildlife as I solved this case from lockup, and you ruined it with your gallant rescue."

"Good to know. Give me a second to add this data into my Learning Jane logbook." A brief glimpse of that lopsided smile. "More jail time for Jane. Got it."

Jane didn't mean to, but she laughed out loud. Oh! How could she let herself find amusement at a time like this? She lightly slapped his chest, thinking to issue a reprimand. Hmm. Was he smuggling rocks under his skin? Because dang. His chest was rock hard.

Cease fondling the agent, Jay Bird. Right. But like she could really blame herself. "Stop being adorable," she scolded as she removed her hands from his torso. "I'm not supposed to enjoy my reentry into society."

"Adorable? Me?" The lopsided grin returned wider...and lingered. "Now that isn't something I've ever heard before."

"Well, then, you aren't hanging around the right people." She grinned back at him; she just couldn't help it. Besides, he'd needed to hear it, to know she recognized the special-ness—the rarity—of his softer side's emergence. To understand his importance to her.

They lapsed into silence after that, neither speaking again. Not until he parked in her driveway, unbuckled, and turned toward her.

"Another chat inside a vehicle. Maybe this one will end better for me, eh?" he teased. "Listen. Before we go inside and you crash—"

"I'm not going to crash," she rushed to interject. Fatigue might have gripped her only moments ago, but fresh energy surged now. They had a murderer to catch.

"—let me tell you what I know about Blake Crawford, the real estate agent," he finished.

Tony had passed along the message, as requested. What an unexpectedly kind thing to do. She nodded, saying, "Yes, please, and thank you. Tell me everything. Leave nothing out."

"For the record," he said, then performed some kind of romantic movie-move to free Jane. They shifted to face each other fully. "I prefer not to explain anything we learned. You'll demand we do something I won't like. Or something that will get me into trouble. Probably both. But. I'm telling you anyway, because you're looking at me with those big, blue eyes."

She was? "Conrad, doing things you don't like has afforded me a hundred percent solve rate so far. Even Robby Waynes has noticed. Why stop such a good thing?"

He grunt-laughed. "I don't want to know how Beau did it, but he got Mr. Crawford's address and did a rundown on his personal history. He lives in Atlanta. Troubled marriage. Collapsing business. Massive debt."

"You have Blake's address?" The day grew better by the second.

"I do," he responded cautiously.

Perfect. "Give me five minutes to shower, scour off the memory of prison—"

"It was jail. There's a difference." He scowled at her. "You had a cot, at least. I had to sleep in a cushionless chair."

"—and change into clean clothes... Wait. What? You slept there?"

He tugged at his shirt collar as red crept along his cheeks, and Jane marveled. For the first time since meeting Special

Agent Conrad Ryan, he appeared uncomfortable. Then he shook it off and cupped her cheek. "Sherrif Moore said you refused to leave. I didn't want you feeling...alone."

He'd spent the entire night in the lobby of the jail-house? For her. Flutters erupted in her stomach. She...he...

No, no. She wouldn't obsess about what that meant right now. Or if it meant anything at all. Or nothing. "After you talk Fiona into making me a stack or twelve of her blueberry pancakes, I'll do you the courtesy of allowing you to drive me to the city. We're going to stake out Blake's place. And do you think it's weird that we're dealing with a Blake and a Jake at the same time?"

He pinched the bridge of his nose. "Jane. People have rhyming names. It isn't a clue."

Right. Of course. People had rhyming names often. Except, this time, it was weird. "And the pancakes?" Fiona was a baking sorceress with the singular power to transform ordinary pancakes into a culinary masterpiece.

Conrad didn't look any less grim. "My answer to every-thing is the same. No pancakes. You aren't getting rewarded for insisting on your own arrest. And no stakeout or interro-gation either. I won't question him. However, I *will* pass the information to Hightower."

"Wow. Jump to conclusions much?" She tsked at him. "I'll be the one asking Blake our list of questions. There's only one ace detective in this car, bud, and it isn't you."

The corners of his mouth twitched. "You're a brat. You know that, right?"

"Maybe." As haughtily as she could manage, she flipped her hair over her shoulder. "I'd rather make the trip with you than without you, and I'm willing to bargain. What if I promise not to approach Blake? To just drive by his house, all innocent-like?"

He laughed outright, the rusty bark that warmed every

inch of her. "You mean you'll be content to stalk the man from a distance, the way you did with Tiffany Hotchkins?"

Speaking of— "Don't forget we have dinner plans on Saturday. We'll call it Operation Gravestone."

His brow cocked. "No stone left unturned?"

"Something like that. We can brainstorm during our road trip." She leaned in and kissed his lips, surprising them both, then darted out of the car and hurried inside the house to prepare.

CHAPTER NINE

"Meet your next fixer upper!"
Diamond City, Nevada - Diamond in the Rough Party
4 Matches Made!

*J*ane fell asleep two minutes after staggering into her bedroom. That meant no blueberry pancakes for her, dang it. Not even plain pancakes. No trip to the city with Conrad. No confrontation with Blake. And she still hadn't checked the photos she'd taken at the *Gold Fever!* exhibit.

On the plus side, she'd learned Beau completed his search of the grounds and he'd never found planted evidence. She must have stopped the Kirklands before they completed their mission. Also on the plus side, Fiona had given her the biggest hug.

Now, however, it was time to rise. With a groan, Jane eased into an upright position on her four-poster bed. Sunlight bathed into her small, somewhat cluttered room, filtering through a window draped by thin, light purple curtains. A cat hammock kept those curtains parted twenty-four seven, allowing Rolex to peer out any time he pleased.

Speaking of, her precious sat on the gorgeous patchwork quilt, crafted with love in shades of lilac, violet and lavender, and licked his belly, a leg extended into the air.

"I'm not gonna draw you like one of my French girls," she teased, scratching him behind the ears. "Did our guests leave?" The house struck her as eerily quiet.

Her phone lit up on the antique nightstand, next to a stack of hats, signaling a new text, but the device emitted no sounds. Ugh. The thing was only a few years old. If she had to fork over a single cent to buy another one, she was gonna be so mad.

She leaned over to swipe up the device and frowned. There were three texts from Tiffany.

Mrs. Hots PMS: *Don't forget! My house, Saturday. 7:00 pm.*

Oh wow. Okay. Until this moment, Jane hadn't realized giving someone a title of 'Possible Murder Suspect' would also reference premenstrual syndrome. She made a quick adjustment, deleting the PMS.

Anyway. There was a picture attached to the message. An admittingly cute selfie of Tiffany and Jake. She smiled at the camera while he kissed her cheek, locks of her dark, shoulder length hair mixing with his lighter strands and streaking over his freshly shaven jaw.

How adorable would Conrad look with Jane's long mane hanging over him?

Focus! Right. She read on.

Mrs. Hots: *You're still coming, right?*

Mrs. Hots: *If you're planning to blow me off, just tell me.*

Had Jane been this irritating when she'd texted and called while under the influence of the thorn apple? Because yikes! Tiffany sure was eager to make this dinner happen. *Too eager* for an apology dinner, perhaps? In books and movies, most people tried to cancel those.

Yeah, this was suspicious. Definitely. Could it be a set-up of some sort? Tiffany and Abigail were super close; the best of friends since elementary school. They must hope to use this dinner to draw Jane out of the house, allowing the Kirklands to come back and finish whatever they'd attempted to do. Probably with Robby in tow.

Well, then. The trio had a big surprise coming. As head of security, Beau would be stalking the grounds, ready to nab them the second they stepped foot on the property.

One way or another, Jane was getting answers.

Other messages awaited her.

Agent Spice: *Not gonna fall asleep? He may say otherwise, but Rolex has been fed. Also, I added my feedback to your case notes. And just in case you're beginning to fall in love with me thanks to my newest gallant deeds—I snore.*

Her heart leaped. This man. Oh, this man. What was she going to do with him?

Beaudyguard: *The goal is to keep you out of jail—you get that, right?*

Fionality: *I'm gonna need some Jane time today. Check your bathroom.*

Her bathroom? Why? Then she spotted the current day and time and executed a movie worthy double take. Wednesday, 7:13. A.M. As in morning. Weed-whacking Wednesday. Which meant she'd slept all yesterday and all night. She still wore her prison uniform—the dress she'd selected for her visit to the museum. Ugh. Usually, she was up and clean and inspecting the grounds by now.

Sighing, she drafted a response to the would-be hostess.

Hi. I apologize for the delay. I was ambushed by a significant life lesson yesterday.

Very excited to see you and Jake on Sat.

Perfect. Send.

Wait. There was an email from Tony in her box. *Subject: My invaluable services.* Jane gasped when she read the accompanying note. You rehired me without a discount. She opened the accompanying attachment and ground her teeth —an invoice for a thirty-second phone call to Beau. $400.

Jane jabbed her fingers at the screen, typing her response. *I will pay you the only wages we ever contractually agreed upon and not a cent more! If you have any further questions, you can contact my other attorney as soon as I hire someone.*

Send.

This was already shaping up to be a terrible day. Rather than reply to her friends while in the midst of a bad mood, she tossed the cell to her pillow, climbed out of bed, and padded to the bathroom, where she found a note from Fiona taped to her mirror. Ah! The reason to check the bathroom.

Blake Crawford is hosting an open house today. Since I've got a sudden burning desire to acquire real estate, we should go, right co-captain?

Oh, what a glorious day! "I love you, Fiona." Forget any weed whacking. Jane rushed back to her phone and texted an acceptance to her dearest, oldest friend in all the world.

A prompt response followed, solidifying their plans to leave in an hour. Jane then sent a group text to her boys. *Stop whatever you're doing! This is a Janergency. Beau, as chief security officer, you are needed immediately. How soon can you get to the Garden? I'll be running an errand with Fiona soon and the Kirklands are still on the loose. Conrad, since you're on vacation, you may remain at my house today, on Rolex duty. FYI he eats at 10 and not a minute later or you will be forced to pay the price.*

Beaudyguard: *Did you really just say JANERGENCY?*

Agent Spice: *You made rock solid plans with me yesterday, then blew me off with a threat that you needed to keep sleeping or people would start to die. Now you expect favors?*

She heard both their teasing tones in her head and rolled her eyes, trying not to smile. But oh, how she liked each man's sense of humor.

Jane: *Yes! I DESERVE favors. I took one for Team Truth yesterday, letting myself fall into a coma.*

Beau and Conrad responded within a millisecond of each other.

Beaudyguard: *How is THAT taking one for the team?*

Agent Spice: *Don't ask her how, Beau. Do not.*

Jane: *I'll tell you how. I made that sacrifice to ensure Captain Jane, your esteemed leader, works at peak capacity for this very moment. What can I say? I'm a giver.*

Again, Beau and Conrad responded within milliseconds.

Beaudyguard: *You make a good point. Give me an hour.*

Agent Spice: *I can be there in half an hour. BTW, I turned your phone to silent. You'll want to fix that before you go. In case I call to ask for Rolex-survival advice.*

Okay, no help for it. The smile broke free as Jane fixed the ringer on her cell and set the device aside.

Rolex met her gaze and seemed to grin–before coughing up a hairball on the bed. Then he blinked at her, as if to say, *Why isn't this cleaned up already?* He hopped from the bed and meowed from the hardwood floor, a demand for a snack.

"Why are you so cute?" Jane demanded.

So much to do before she left. Wash the sheets. Look over the account books for the graveyard trust and issue Tony a check for twenty dollars, far more than their agreed upon rate for any consultation. Finally look over the photos from the *Gold Fever!* exhibit and compare them to the original photos of her donation. Had Abigail and Robby switched documents as Ana had believed?

First, though, Jane planned to luxuriate in a shower hot enough to peel the flesh from her bones and scrub off the slammer. New day, clean slate.

~

JANE AND FIONA walked arm-in-arm around a cute bungalow in Atlanta's Candler Park, pretending to enjoy this, whatever it was, and that thing, or some other.

Blake Crawford, here in the flesh.

He was conducting a tour of the home, allowing Jane to study him at her leisure. He was almost six feet. Thirty-nine years-old, with dark hair and pale skin, plus a bushel of fine lines around his eyes and a slight bump in the bridge of his nose. A modern-day bruiser. Stress emanated from him.

Ana had claimed this man had drained Robby Wayne's bank accounts. Had he?

Though he was in the middle of a messy divorce, according to Beau's top-secret research, Blake still wore his wedding ring.

"He's a rubber band soon to pop," Fiona whispered to her. "Any second now. Just you wait and see."

"That might be because you keep asking him questions," Jane whispered back.

"If that's too bothersome for him, he's working the wrong job." Another whisper before Fiona blurted her next question for the entire group to hear. "What can you tell me about the crown molding? Is it all original or did sections get replaced? And do you think the replacements were made because of mold?"

When they'd first signed on for the tour, Jane had thought to observe Blake in his natural habitat, nothing more, then ask him to join her for drinks to discuss the offer she wouldn't be making. She could then (masterfully) weave in questions featuring Ana and his alleged thievery.

Now Jane would be lucky to last until the end of the walk-through. Blake's cheeks flushed, nearing a hue some might call fire engine red.

"There is no mold," he grated before resuming his presentation. "Look at the size of this veranda. Yes, it blocks some of the natural light, but imagine sipping iced tea as you watch the sunset. In fact, the bungalow style totally captures and maximizes light with the high set of the windows. I think you'll really love the picturesque bay window in the master." He herded them into the next bedroom.

Sunlight filled the room, tinted by the lovely stained glass in a geometric design.

"Ooh," Jane couldn't help but sigh. "Very pretty." Her phone dinged, and she checked the screen. A text from Tony, asking if she had caused any other legal messes in need of clean up.

She ground her teeth. He was either taunting her or in desperate need of money. Or both.

Fiona elbowed her in the ribs, and Jane put her phone away. The open house. Right. *You're a hard-nosed detective, pretending not to be charmed by walls painted in a muted sage and built-in bookcases.* Although, honestly, the maple woodwork—stained a gorgeous burnt umber—was stunning. Maybe she could host another paid tour soon and earn enough to make updates at the cottage.

There were only six other people on the walk-through, but Jane's attention kept returning to a young couple who might be stealing knickknacks from artfully staged rooms. Which meant Jane might be minutes from solving her second case—Cemetery Girl and the House Tour Bandits. The Crooked House Hunter? Whatever. She could come up with a better name later.

"I skimmed a few videos from home inspectors this morning, so I'm one hundred percent confident I know what I'm talking about," Fiona remarked, catching Jane's attention. "I'd stake my life on it—this house once had termites." She wrinkled her nose. "A total infestation, most likely."

"What?" gasped one of the women. Legitimately interested or playing the angle? Jane couldn't tell.

The realtor rushed to the couple, his hands lifted in innocence. "No termites have been found anywhere in the structure."

Fiona gave him a *who are you trying to fool?* expression. "Well. Not officially."

Blake attempted to laugh off his growing fury while a vein throbbed in the center of his brow. "Again. There's been no mold or termites."

"To be sure, we should talk to the neighbors." Fiona smiled at him, all earnestness and innocence. "What are they like, anyway? I bet they'll know why the owners are leaving." She sucked in a breath, facing Jane. "Do you think ghosts live here?"

"There are no ghosts. No mold, no termites. There's nothing wrong with the house," Blake bellowed. And like that, his calm shattered. Veins popped out alongside his neck too. He panted his breaths as he pointed to the door. "Get out. Just get out. The tour is over."

Wow. Jane wondered if his rhyming buddy Jake ever reacted as volatile as this.

The rest of the viewers raced out as if their feet were on fire. Jane stayed put because Fiona stayed put. Leave a friend behind? Never!

"Please, just go," Blake said, defeated. Tension and strain radiated from him as he slumped into a charcoal mid-century modern armchair, rumpling the once perfectly fluffed throw pillow.

Fiona slipped into doting grandmother mode and glided over to pat him on the head. "There, there, sugar. You're going through a bit of trouble, aren't you? Well, Granny Fee is here to help. Tell me everything, and I'll share with you what I'd tell my grandson, if he were in your situation."

Goodness gracious. If drilling past his defenses to reach the misery of the matter worked, Fiona deserved an award. Amateur Sleuth of the Day.

Outrage, suspicion, and indecision played over Blake's features before he crumbled. "Someone stole my ID and emptied my bank accounts. I'm poised at the brink of ruin, losing everything I love, one thing at a time."

Surprised, Jane shuffled back a step. So, this guy wasn't the thief? If he was telling the truth, he was the victim.

Was he? She thought…yes. His misery and upset struck her as genuine. Which meant he was just a guy in desperate need of a friend, someone willing to listen without censure. Unless he had recognized Jane because he'd cased the cemetery and planned the best way to frame her for Ana's death and now played the role of innocent.

Or Ana had done the stealing herself and blamed him. Or Robby had lied because he was the thief.

Robby the Robber. It just fit.

"That's truly awful." Fiona petted Blake's hair. "But there's more, isn't there, sugar?"

"Oh, yeah." He laughed without humor. "My wife thinks I spent the money on another woman. As if I would ever. Yes, I considered it once, but I didn't do anything. Clara is leaving me anyway. Someone *must* have stolen my ID," he repeated, growing angry again. "That's the only explanation. I thought I lost it, so I got a new one. But the thief must have used the old one, pretending to be me. Because I did *not* walk into my bank and withdraw every cent I own. I don't care what the footage shows." He plowed a hand through his hair. "I didn't do it."

Well. He certainly appeared sincere. And if he *was*?

"Footage?" Jane asked.

"Bank cameras show I was there. But I wasn't," he insisted.

"I'm sorry for your troubles," Fiona said, all grandmotherly comfort. "And I'm sorry there's nothing I can say to make it better. Except this. If you've ever had a hankering for older gals, you could go out and find yourself a new woman. A sugar momma. Perhaps a lady I know. Her name is Irma."

Jane pinched the bridge of her nose. Fiona and her matchmaking tendencies. She just couldn't resist, could she?

"I want my wife back," Blake said.

"Understandable," Fiona replied. "But if you change your mind, Irma would be a real confidence booster *and* help you get back on your feet. Then all your worries would disappear."

At least for a little while, Jane mused. But back to the case. How could cameras show Blake in the bank, if he hadn't been there? The answer eluded her. She only knew there was something here, and as the speed dating slogan prompted, she must only dig deeper to find the gold.

CHAPTER TEN

"Love at first heart leap!"
Lovers Leap, California - Leap Into Love Bash
49 Matches Made!

*C*onrad was folding a ladder on the cottage porch, bathed in golden sunlight as Fiona parked in the driveway. His well-worn jeans had a rip at the knee. A black crewneck T-shirt said this was a casual, carefree moment, but looking at him Jane felt...not casual.

"Don't make that little sighing sound when he's within earshot," Fiona warned. "It's like honey to bears. Right now, you've got your bear all caged up nice and tight. But that can change in an instant."

Jane laughed as she reached for the door handle. "Why is he a bear in this scenario?"

"As if you don't know." Fiona winked. "And for the record, fun things can happen when a bear gets free."

"Yes, but carnage can happen too."

They emerged from the sports car, entering the warm evening light. Beau rounded the corner. Heading up the porch steps, he wiped his dirty hands together in a job well done.

"C'mon." Fiona waved her forward. "Our men look hungry."

"Starved," Beau agreed.

Conrad peered at Jane with heat. "Ravenous."

Shivers slipped over her spine. "Why don't I whip something up quick from whatever I've got in the fridge?" She might have peered at her special agent a little too long as she climbed the steps. "It's the least I can do to thank you guys for holding down the fort while we ran that, um, errand."

He traced his tongue over straight white teeth and pushed open the front door for Fiona. His gaze remained locked on Jane. "You attended an open house in Atlanta, did you?"

"Oh...well...um." She soared into the cottage on Fiona's heels and made a beeline for the kitchen, calling, "I should start cooking."

She hustled from the yellow fridge with a plethora of magnets to the counter and stove, gathering pots and pans along the way. When she dropped a piece of cheese on the black-and-white checkered floor, Rolex swooped in and snagged it. Was there any animal more adorable?

Soon the scent of pan-fried chicken, mashed potatoes, greens, corn pone, buttermilk biscuits and peppered-bacon gravy filled her cottage. Just the basics. As she worked, Conrad went over his case notes with her, solidifying her belief the speed dating/big break served as the catalyst for Ana's murder.

When Jane finished the last dish, the group gathered at the dining room table and dug in. Everyone politely passed plates and bowls back and forth while Jane and Fiona explained what they'd learned from Blake.

"Were there any impromptu visits from the Kirklands

while we were away?" Jane asked, glancing between Conrad and Beau.

Beau answered her with a lifted brow. "While I patrolled the grounds? No."

Excellent. Jane returned her attention to Conrad. "Thanks for making sure Rolex ate yesterday and today. You saved me hours of whining."

He spooned another serving of mashed potatoes. "I deserve a medal for my bravery. He hissed non-stop."

"Yes, but did he scratch you?" she asked.

"Not more than a dozen times."

"So hardly at all." What sweet progress. "I'd say your medal of bravery needs to be downgraded to a participation certificate."

He snorted. "Brat."

"I agree with Jane." Fiona leveled her fork at him. "You're growing on the little darling, Conrad."

"Little darling?" he echoed. "Are you referring to Jane or the hellcat?"

"Both, I bet." Beau buttered a biscuit. "So. You two met the real estate guy. Do you think he's the one who stole from Robby and framed Ana?"

"Never in a trillion years," Fiona burst out. "That poor boy is heartbroken. Ana was wrong to accuse him of a crime he didn't commit. Wrong I tell you!" She added the last while waving her knife around.

The men stared at the older gal as if she'd grown a second head.

"Fiona is passionate about her opinions," Jane explained before sipping her sweet tea.

Conrad placed his fork on his empty plate and stared at Jane, then Fiona, then back at Jane. "You're both adrenaline junkies, aren't you?"

"Us?" Jane sputtered.

"Who can say, really?" Fiona pushed the platter of chicken closer to him. Her eyes twinkled, making her look years younger and more carefree. The way she used to look when Grandma Lily still lived.

See? This investigation was good for her, too.

"Here's the real question," Jane continued. "Did Ana accuse Blake because of false evidence against him or on purpose? If she did it on purpose, I have to wonder if Ana herself is the Savings and Loans Thief—villain name pending—and she blamed Blake to cover her own tracks."

"And if it was because of false evidence, as I suspect?" Conrad asked, draping his napkin over his plate to signal there'd be no third helping of food.

"Then Ana might not be the Savings and Loans Thief." *Well, that circled back to nowhere fast, didn't it?* "Why do you think Ana is innocent?"

He shrugged. "Robby strikes me as the lying type."

"Agreed," Beau said. "Him and everyone else."

"Don't you worry. Team Truth will prevail." Jane shook her fist toward the ceiling. "And Beau, I like where your head's at—suspect everyone, especially the Waynes. Maybe Robby used Ana to steal Blake's money, then turned around and blamed Ana for robbing him, a crime no one had committed. Then, when Ana began to figure out the scheme, bam. Bye-bye hard-hitting journalist."

What was it the real estate agent had said concerning the bank footage? He was there, but not there.

Robby was close in height with a similar hair color. Maybe he'd strolled into the bank pretending to be Blake and simply withdrawn the money. No muss, no fuss. Though why go to so much trouble and risk, putting your reputation on the line for a few, what? Thousand dollars?

Fiona tossed her napkin on the table and stood. "All right,

everyone. I believe it's time to say bye-bye to the leftovers, and get these dishes washed."

Beau shoved back his chair. "I can handle that."

"I'll help him," Conrad said, only to wink at Jane. "To be honest, I'll just stand there while he does all the work, so get that dreamy glaze out of your eyes."

She almost laughed as he walked away.

"What nice young men." Fiona winked at Jane, as if she had successfully executed a complex plan. "Be a dear and grab the yarn, hon. We're running dangerously low on funny bunnies for Sunbeam Children's Home."

As the boys puttered around the kitchen, Fiona and Jane settled in the living room with Rolex to knit. Fiona occupied her usual chair near the hearth. Jane took the couch for once, hoping a certain someone chose the spot at her side.

"You can't exchange two nickels for a dime and think you're rich," Fiona said under her breath. "And that's a fact."

"What does that even mean?" Jane replied with a matching volume. "First bears, now pocket change."

"You know dang good and well what it means. You keep upping the ante. Soon, play time will end."

Conrad and Beau strode into the living room, earning hisses from Rolex, who sat on the coffee table. The perfect interruption because she'd had no idea how to reply. Upping the ante?

She held her breath. Would Conrad...

He claimed the spot right next to her. Like, right, right next to her, with no space between them, and draped a muscular arm behind her. His decadent heat poured over her like honey, and her needle slipped on the strings of her half-made rabbit.

"I love that you make these." A slow smile bloomed on his rugged face, stealing her breath.

A promise lurking in the dark depths of his eyes left her

stomach fluttering. "Knitting is what does it for you, huh?" she teased.

"Yes. Who knew?" He leaned closer and tweaked the tip of her nose. "No, my little brother had a toy just like it. A gift waiting on his bed in a group home." He rubbed at his chin, seeming to get lost in his thoughts and grow a touch sad, which made her chest tighten.

Instead of spewing out curses, as usual, Jane thrust the knitting needles into his hands. "Here. I'll show you how to make one."

She helped him properly angle his knitting needles, surprised to find he had nimble fingers—a thought she would not let herself pursue. "Yes. Like that. Keep it up, and we might be able to tell you made a rabbit instead of accidentally sewing two socks together."

"Funny girl," he said, his gaze lingering on her lips for a moment.

Fiona made a snorting sound from her rocker; a sound Beau mimicked from the rocker next to hers. "Don't let her tease you. A few of Jane's funny bunnies have had four arms and no ears."

"I'm sure the kids loved them," Conrad said, his voice low. "But there's no way anyone will love my monster." He missed a stitch and gave a mock growl. "When I had a garage, I put old car engines back together in my spare time. Why is this so difficult?"

He enjoyed rebuilding car engines? Jane almost smiled. She felt as if she were in the middle of an Introduction to Conrad Ryan class—and passing the prerequisite!

Before he caught her staring dreamily at him, she looked away. Wait. Her living room... Something struck her as different. Different but also the same. What...where—the drapes, she realized. Someone had patched and re-hung the curtains Rolex destroyed the day Jane found Ana. Three someones, no doubt.

If that wasn't the sweetest thing anyone had ever done.

"Thanks, y'all. The curtains look amazing." Jane threw herself at Conrad for a hug he returned, then jumped up and skipped over to kiss Fiona's cheek and squeeze Beau's shoulder. "You guys are the best."

"We know," the trio said in unison, as if they'd rehearsed it.

Everyone chuckled as she scratched Rolex behind the ears and returned to her section of the couch. Her precious angel looked like a gargoyle, now that he'd stopped hissing.

Jane cooed praises as the agent worked the needles through the threads, bringing everything together as perfectly as a key in a lock—key! "Conrad, I meant to ask earlier but do you happen to know why Ana carried a golden key shaped like a shovel in her purse?"

"I do. It's for a locker at the Gold Rush Museum. People store their shoes and socks in a locker and sift through piles of sand. I think she went there to spy on Robby."

"Really?" How disappointing. That wasn't quite the scandal Jane had anticipated. "The museum offers literal gold digging? I've visited the museum twice in a matter of weeks and had no idea."

"That's because you have tunnel vision," Fiona said without glancing up from her toy. "You get your eye set on a prize and you can't see anything else."

Jane shrugged. "What about the mini hammer associated with the fire department?" Hey, look at that? She could mention AHFD out loud without blanching. Her ex, Christopher, had dumped her like she was a hot potato. For no reason! One day he'd just stopped speaking to her.

"Volunteer firefighters offered a trade three years ago," Conrad explained. "Donate five soup cans to the local food bank and receive the hammer to store in your vehicle. It's for if you need to make an emergency break-out."

Oh. "And the, um, bagged panties?"

"A clean pair for an overnight stay somewhere other than home."

"I see." Her cheeks heated. Okay, so, forget the items in Ana's purse. "She was seeing someone after her breakup with Robby?"

"Not that we can tell. She often did overnight surveillance on the people in town."

Yeah. That tracked. But dang it. She was getting nowhere fast. Time for an abrupt turn. "Let's say I'm a thief, and I want to withdraw someone's money while pretending to be them," she said, and Conrad groaned. "What type of ID would I need to clean out their bank account?"

"Just a computer," Beau piped up from his chair as he crafted a piglet. How were both the guys better at knitting these toys on their very first attempt when Jane had been doing this for years? "Whose money do you want and by when?"

Conrad released the needles and massaged his nape, a man who seemed to have lost track of his life a few miles back.

"No, I mean, if you aren't able to hack into programs or whatever." She started a new toy of her own. Maybe the thief —The Robber—knew computers, maybe he didn't. And she hadn't forgotten about the breach of her own security feed. "If you actually go inside the bank, expecting to be filmed."

"Depends on the amount of cash being withdrawn, I think." Fiona shrugged. "My first husband—God rest his soul —used to complain when he didn't have to jump through hoops to access his money. No hoops, no protections."

Conrad nodded. "Anything over ten grand, the bank has to report to the government. And in a town as small as this one? Everyone knows everyone. No one can pretend to be someone else."

So where did Robby bank?

"The problem with larger towns," Beau said, "you'd have to find someone who looks like you, steal their ID, and learn some basic information. That takes time and commitment. Too much time and commitment for a small payout."

Unless your motive wasn't money but revenge. Or to shut up a reporter. If Robby had decided to off Ana for one of her stories, he would have planned ahead. Picked a scapegoat. Jane and/or Blake. Or Jake. A main suspect and a spare. A just in case. And dang it, there must be something to those rhyming names, no matter what Conrad said.

So, the real question was: What did Robby have to hide?

Jane *needed* more information. A sit down with Ana herself. Which, granted, seemed impossible, considering the journalist was dead and all. But honestly, call Jane an optimist, but she still had hope. A way could be made, even when there appeared to be no path. How many conversations had she, Grandma Lily, and Pops enjoyed since they'd died? Countless. Had they ever responded? No. But it didn't make the discussions any less affirming.

"Uh-oh. I know that look." Conrad gently chucked her under her chin. He appeared to be fighting a smile as he toyed with the ends of her hair. "Your nose wrinkles when you get lost in your head. So who's your main suspect and why? Still the Waynes or someone different?"

Jane did not want to admit the truth. Because yes, more and more she was certain the pair had everything to do with this. Her two-man protection crew would tell her that Abigail, Robby and Landon could accuse her of stalking or something equally nefarious if ever she confronted them, then bend the truth to prove it. But admit the truth she did, risking a scolding. Better safe than sorry this time around.

Personal growth sucked sometimes.

"During the last case," she said, "Abigail became convinced I'm hiding a fortune in the cemetery. What if the motive behind all of this is just that? The gold. If the Waynes siblings can get me locked away for life for a murder I didn't commit, they can gain easy access to the Garden. An elaborate set up with an expected payoff."

"It's possible," Conrad allowed. "I'll talk to Hightower."

"For the record," Beau said, "if the bank in the larger town is crowded, you just need the right hair, clothes and build to pass as someone else for an overworked teller. Most people see only what they expect to see. More than that, you don't have to be a whiz with the latest in camera tech to manipulate what people observe. If you knew their placement and angled yourself accordingly, you could mask most differences."

Fiona made a twittering sound. "All those instagrammers have a leg up already."

So. With the right person, it could be done. "This is valuable information, thank you."

Were they correct? Did people only see what they wanted to see? In person and on camera? Someone would catch the differences between the real and the fake. Like, if some strange woman dressed up as Jane went to her bank to withdraw her (meager) funds, a teller or other official would notice she wasn't who she said she was. Surely!

Maybe, maybe not. But there was a way to find out...

An idea percolated. An approach to test her theory. Kind of. Adequate, anyway. "Has Ana's home been cleared for entry?" she asked as casually as she was able.

"It has," Conrad offered, hesitant as he picked up his needles and got back to work. "Why?"

"Oh. I, uhh—" Well. She refused to lie, but she also

refused to admit this particular truth. Baby steps! So where did that leave her?

Fiona rose to her feet. "Oh goodnessdear, look at the time. It's late, and Jane needs her beauty rest. I'll just take that knitting," she said, plucking needles, toys and yarn from the boys.

Conrad and Beau stood, both clearly confused by the abrupt change. No, not confused. Suspicious.

"Jane, you're not thinking—" Conrad began.

"Don't you dare even consider—" Beau started.

"Yes, yes. You can warn her all you like tomorrow." Her friend winked before shooing the boys to the door.

They walked toward their cars, dazed and in no hurry to leave.

Fiona waved her arms. "Someone check my car. Be sure to neutralize any murderers who are waiting inside to kill me. I'll be along in a jiff." She hung back long enough to kiss Jane's cheek and mutter, "I'm on board with your plan. You get the clothes, and I'll find the wig."

Best friends were amazing!

The front door closed behind Fiona, leaving Jane and Rolex alone. Her furry beastie circled around her feet until she picked him up and hugged him close. "I don't think the world is ready for my sting operation, baby, but I am." She grinned. "Tomorrow, I become Ana."

Only moments later, hinges squeaked, the front door opening once again. She stood frozen.

Conrad stuck his head inside the foyer, his expression grave as he met her gaze. "Please think through what you're planning. If you go through with it, whatever it is, you'll get yourself into trouble. Or me. Or both of us. Probably both of us. Just…remember the last case. You ended up drugged. You could have been hurt."

He said no more, just disappeared, shutting the door

behind him. Jane stood in place, her heart thundering, a million thoughts racing through her mind. The curse. Their doom. Her plan. Her certainty that she could prove him wrong. Besides, he admired Hightower's obsessive determination. Now, he could admire Jane's.

CHAPTER ELEVEN

"Mix and match!"
Cupid, Iowa - Making Your Acquaintance Social
12 Matches Made

*J*ane's excitement wasn't nearly as palpable the next morning. *Too tired.* She'd tossed and turned all night.

A knock sounded at the door just as she smashed a pillow over her head, hoping to steal an extra ten hours of sleep. Groaning, she crawled out of bed and padded to the front door wearing the nightgown and robe Fiona had sewn her for Christmas, Rolex on her heels.

Beau stood on the porch, wearing his usual white T-shirt and jeans, haloed by sunlight and holding a thermos. "Ready to guard the grounds against shovel-carrying intruders, boss. By the way, my friends are due to arrive any day now. Okay if I bring them by the cemetery for a look around?"

Rolex hissed at him.

"Of course," she said, rubbing tired eyes before she waved him inside. "I'll prepare you guys a meal. Just get me a list of everyone's favorite foods, desserts, and dietary restrictions. A brief overview of their personality types and romantic history wouldn't be amiss, either."

He swept past her, bringing the scent of roasted coffee beans with him. "Just quote unquote whip a little something up for us, like usual. They'll love it."

What a sweet thing to say. "So where is Conrad?" The question spilled out before she could stop it.

"You should have a text from him. He drove back to the city, but he plans to return to Aurelian Hills on Saturday for your dinner with Tiffany."

Saturday. Judgment Day. The rendering of Jane's verdict. Was the widow Hotchkins helping Abigail with her crimes against the cemetery or not? Had they worked together to harm Ana?

"Did he return to the office?" After last night's concern... did he hope to distance himself from Jane for a little while?

"He didn't say."

Hmm. She needed to check her phone. "Make yourself at home while I prepare for the day." She hurried to her bedroom and shut herself inside. After cleaning up, she felt alive at least. Jane donned a pretty, blue dress, and checked her phone.

Only one text waited for her, and it wasn't from Conrad, but Tony. How disappointing. What did this lack of communication mean?

Tremors plagued her as she deciphered the attorney's many misspellings. *I gipe you of ro jail* had to mean *I hope you go to jail.*

Sent during a night of drinking too much? His true feelings on the matter?

Well, well. Tony Miller had just bought himself a tick right back up to the top of her list.

Feeling somewhat alive again, Jane selected a sunhat and

returned to Beau, who sat on the living room couch, his head bent over his phone. With his broad shoulders and rock-solid frame, he had seemed too big for her small cottage at first. Yet, he'd carved out a place for himself with zero fuss.

Beau stood when she entered the room. "Ready for your morning rounds?"

She patted the pocket of her dress, making sure she'd remembered to grab a notepad and pen. "Ready."

He led her into the surprisingly cool morning and remained at her side as they scoured the grounds, with Rolex sticking to their heels. While she kept a running list of necessary chores, he remained on the lookout for intruders and any signs of a disturbance.

When they passed Tree, the glorious magnolia with sage advice, she wished it would come alive and tell her how to keep Conrad.

She must have stared a little too long because Beau laughed and said, "Is this the infamous wise one Fiona told me about? Want to introduce me?"

"Yes, it is, and no, I do not," she responded with a prim tone, earning a snicker.

As they made their way back to the cottage, he kicked a pebble, drawing her attention to his feet. When she noticed the expensive cut of his boots, a question bubbled up in her mind.

"Beau, we're friends, which means we have no personal boundaries," she began. "So I'm just gonna ask you the nosiest question of all time. You can refuse to answer, and I won't be upset. For very long. But. Are you rich? Okay, two questions. If you *are* rich, how'd you make your money?" When he'd lived in town as a kid, his family had seemed, well, as poor as hers. If not poorer. "I take up most of your time and pay you pennies, if you even deign to cash your checks, yet you bought a place on Prospect Street. Do you have some kind of secret life?"

Tone cautious, he asked, "Are you hinting that you believe I stole from someone?"

"Goodness no! Nothing like that. Your heart is too soft for crime."

"My heart...is soft?" he said, then shook his head as if he'd misheard her.

"I'm asking if you secretly work as a romance novel cover model in your spare time." The perfect job for him. "Or maybe you went a step further and wrote a bestselling military thriller under a pen name. Perhaps a relative left you a first edition of a novel and you sold it for millions at auction."

His brow wrinkled, sunlight glinting off his golden hair. "Why do all of your ideas for me revolve around books?"

"Are you kidding? It's your vibe. Very straight from the pages of a sizzling adventure."

He snorted as they crested a hill, the cottage coming into view. "My situation is complicated. I do have money. A lot of it. But I'd like to leave it at that."

"Fair enough." Except now she was even *more* curious. Did he think she'd treat him differently? Well, think again. "Just understand that this makes me want to find you a girlfriend faster." A companion he trusted with his secrets. Then he might not feel so alone. And he did feel alone. She sensed it—because she felt that way at times, too.

"Jane," he said with a groan.

Intending to tell her to forget about setting him up? Too bad. "I have some errands to run, and you have some patrolling to do." She skipped ahead of him, calling, "If the Kirklands show up, you are authorized to use full force."

"Or I can let them do what they want and catch them in the act."

"Don't be silly. I'm a hardened criminal who has spent time behind bars now. Catch them before they do anything and show no mercy." She bumped her fist toward the sky as she climbed the porch steps. "Okay, bye."

"What am I gonna do with you?" he called. "By the way, do not do what you're planning. It won't end well."

"Inside the house now. Can't hear you." The front door slammed behind her. She gathered her purse and a little extra cash from her emergency fund. After feeding and kissing Rolex, she headed to the hearse, Beau nowhere in sight.

Wait. Her phone. She'd left it on her nightstand.

Sure enough, there was a text from Conrad. Finally!

Agent Spice: *Miss me today.*

Relieved to the core of her being, she kind of hugged the cell to her chest before typing a response. *Are you back at work?*

Agent Spice: *Not yet. Just have to handle some things at home.*

What kind of things? So badly she wanted to ask. Which meant she shouldn't. And really, she wasn't sure she had the right, considering she'd been keeping him at a distance while he'd only tried to get closer to her.

Her relief dried up as she dropped the phone in her purse.

Thankfully, the drive to town proved uneventful, far different from her last trip. A few stops to pick up everything she thought she might need took longer than expected. But then, she had a very specific shopping list.

Once she had purchased every item, she drove to Fiona's house in Bedrock, a small neighborhood filled with southern craftsmans and folksy Victorians right off Main Street. After her first and second husbands had died, she'd sold her farm outside of the city to be closer to her favorite coffee and sandwich shops.

Fiona waved her inside with a ready and eager smile, but quickly drew the curtain as soon as they were sealed inside. They intended to turn Jane into the long-lost sister of Tatiana Irons, and search the journalist's home.

"What are you hunting for at Ana's, exactly?" Fiona asked as they got started.

"Anything pointing to the speed daters, the Waynes, the Hotchkins or Tony Miller." Let Operation Gravestone commence.

~

JANE ADJUSTED AN ITCHY, strawberry blonde wig and plowed on with her rehearsed story. "So, you see, I am Ana's long, lost sister—"

"Let me stop you there, because I don't actually care," Ana's neighbor said, a young woman with a baby on her hip and two toddlers at her calves. "I have a spare key to her place. After the landlord charged her forty bucks for an unlock, we exchanged keys. Well, once I signed an NDA, provided a drop of blood and a full set of fingerprints."

"Really?"

"No, but almost. I'll grab it for you. Here." She shifted the child into Jane's unsuspecting arms, then popped inside the apartment, taking the toddlers with her.

The baby's hair was scooped into a ponytail high on her head and framed by a pretty pink bow. She looked at Jane with wide-eyed fascination. Then one tiny hand gripped a hank of Jane's fake locks and tugged.

The wig shifted too far to the right, and Fiona rushed to help straighten the voluminous hairpiece before Ana's neighbor returned.

"I knew the third time would be the charm," her friend said.

GENA SHOWALTER & JILL MONROE

They'd spoken to two others who'd all but slammed the door in their faces.

"Here you go," the mother said, claiming her child and slapping the key in Jane's palm. "I'll miss Ana. She was fun. I can't tell you how many times she babysat my trio of heck-beasts when I had to work late or brought over a bottle of wine to share with me. She certainly had a lot of interesting stories featuring the people in this town."

Having neighbors sounded lovely. "That she did."

Jane waved as the door shut, then she and Fiona aimed for the correct apartment. There might be something wonderfully or terribly insidious to this dress-up and pretend thing, after all. A twist of the key, and the lock clicked. The door to Ana's place snickered open.

"Wow. Gotta say, this was almost too easy," Fiona said with a shudder.

"I was just thinking the same thing. But the worst part is, I didn't even get to finish my heartfelt story of being sepa-rated from my dearly departed older sister through no fault of my own."

Okay. Mind on the mission. Jane really hoped to find a crime board outlining everything Ana had investigated. What a timesaver that would be. "While I search for clues, you wait downstairs in the lobby to act as my lookout."

"Ten-four. If any lawmen or dubious characters show up while you're searching for those clues, I'll contact you imme-diately. You get a text from me, you get out of there, okay? Even if the text is garbled nonsense because I'm typing without looking while I do some distracting."

"No problem. And thank you." Jane kissed her cheek before slipping inside the one bedroom and closing the door behind her. Rather than turn on the lights, she used the flash-light on her phone for illumination.

As she prowled through the home, she nearly tripped

over a couple stacks of boxes. Ana's real family must have started the heart-wrenching process of packing up her stuff.

The would-be journalist had decorated her apartment in an eclectic style of mismatched...everything. Everything seemed to belong to a different design style. The common theme: pops of color. From the bright yellow and teal comforter to the red sofa with silver nail heads and pink throw pillows.

In a section cordoned off with hanging cloth, Jane found the "office." Over a collapsible wall-desk, twinkle lights illuminated a cork bulletin board covered with photos.

Jackpot. Most of the pictures were printed from a social media page and featured men Jane had never met, in typical profile poses. Their ages ranged from twenty to forty. Ana had written names, dates, and locations on the back of each.

Jane used her phone to record a video of the photos. Hey! There was Robby. She snatched the printout off the tack, bringing the image closer to her face. Yep. Definitely Robby. He sat on a boat, grinning, and holding up a fish he'd caught.

Another photo caught her eye. Blake. Oh! And there was another of Blake. In the first, he had his arm wrapped around a petite brunette at a formal event. He wore a suit and tie: she wore a black gown. In the other photo, the same brunette kissed his chin while they lay in bed. An early morning selfie. Both were smiling.

The wife? Or the alleged girlfriend he denied having?

Oh, and there was another of Robby. And Tony. Another of Tony with his ex-wife Emma. Even handsome, golden Jake Stephenson was mixed in—but not with his fiancée Tiffany. No, he had his lips pressed into the cheek of a completely different brunette. And also a blonde.

Were the other women the reason Jake had sought a fresh start in a new town? Had he cheated on one with the other, earning the wrath of both? Or were all these people innocent?

Jane stepped back and took in the full impact of the bulletin board. There was a (slight) possibility Ana had been a stalker rather than a journalist. But had she also been a thief? Had she targeted these men and paid a lookalike to drain their accounts? Or had she chased the thief?

In the next room, hinges squeaked. Someone had just opened a door. Fiona was supposed to stay in the lobby and text her if there was a problem. But her friend might not recognize one of Ana's actual family members.

Jane powered off the flashlight on her phone, going still. Heart thudding, she backed into a shadowed corner and crouched.

"—that you are breaking and entering right now, sheriff," Fiona was saying.

Relief deluged Jane, and she straightened, stepping past the cloth divider. Except, what did her friend mean, *sheriff?*

"I told you to stay behind me, Fee," a deep, *familiar* voice proclaimed, all but dripping with exasperation. Oh yes. The sheriff indeed. "I didn't pull my deputy off this to let you and Jane finish doing whatever it is you're doing."

Fiona dashed toward the office, her dark eyes wide. When she spotted Jane, she winced in apology. "I got distracted by his tush and had to race into the elevator with him," she whispered, rushing over. "There was no stopping him. But don't worry, hon. There's a way out of this, I'm sure of it."

Oh no, no, no. But there was nowhere to hide. Thumping footsteps sounded as Sheriff Moore appeared. He tilted back his Stetson and hooked his thumbs in the waist of his pants.

"Ladies," he said, looking from one to the other. "A neighbor called to let me know there's someone impersonating Ana's sister."

Well. Thank goodness all of Jane's neighbors were dead. The living ones sucked.

"Would you believe me if I lied and said I only hoped to grab the photos Ana borrowed from me and never returned?" Jane asked with a grimace. She'd hoped to prove Conrad wrong; looked like she was about to prove him right.

"No, ma'am." He freed a pair of cuffs from his belt.

"Did you bring only one pair, Sheriff?" Fiona sounded genuinely intrigued as she held out her wrists. "And are you taking suggestions for who gets to wear them?"

He drew in a deep breath, then exhaled heavily. "You both have the right to remain silent, and I suggest you utilize it."

CHAPTER TWELVE

"Speak and Spark!"
Valentine, New Jersey - Instant Connection Reception
25 Matches Made

Using her hip, Jane pressed the button to trigger the automatic door to Conrad's condo. She stepped off the sidewalk and through the glass entrance, balancing a foil casserole dish in her arms. She'd had no idea he lived in the Montgomery. Once an opulent five-story department store built in the 1920s, it had fallen into disrepair until developers restored the building to its former glory a few years back, even keeping the fun art deco style.

As she strolled to the concierge desk, her high heels clicked on the parquet floors, which appeared original to the building. Sleek geometric murals decorated the walls of a circular lobby, with rounded columns painted a deep yellow. Dramatic chandeliers filled the space with muted light and hung from a ceiling that must be at least twenty feet high.

"How may I help you?" asked a man stationed at an imposing mahogany desk. Behind him were black and white tile inlays and gold accents. Stunning. Intimidating. So not Jane.

She eyed the elevator, then the exit. The scent of made-from-scratch grits and sausage casserole infused the air. So at odds with the fragrance of cleaners layering her every inhalation.

Should she just go home?

"Ma'am?" he prompted.

"I'm here to see Conrad Ryan, but I think I'll—"

"It will be my honor to announce you," he said, already picking up the phone.

The words had been framed oh, so politely, but the man's tone rang firm. She glanced at the exit one last time. Making a break for it would be ridiculous now.

"Are you Ms. Ladling?" he asked, covering the receiver.

She nodded, grateful and relieved that Conrad hadn't expected a different woman. That would have been humiliating.

Why run, anyway? Surely this culinary masterpiece would make up for all the trouble she'd caused the agent—her boyfriend—yesterday. If not the dish, then Jane's attire. She'd worn her "apology dress." A pink beauty with a corset top and flared, calf-length skirt, the soft fabric covered in darker hearts.

Sheriff Moore hadn't freed Jane and her cohort until after he'd called the agent.

Uh... Maybe she should return to the cottage, after all. If Conrad had wanted to see her, he would have driven to Aurelian Hills. Right? He hadn't even called or texted to gloat. Meaning...

He'd probably washed his hands of her for real this time and hoped for a clean break. Coming here was dumb.

Her stomach twisted, and she stepped back, preparing to pivot. That exit looked better and better. The elevator dinged, its doors sliding open. Too late. Conrad emerged, entering the lobby with a cell phone pressed to his ear.

Her breath caught, and her heart thudded. He looked good. Really good. Like, really, really, *really* good. His dark hair was messy, his gorgeous amber irises bright. A plain black T-shirt with the GBH logo molded to sculpted muscles, displayed many of his arm tattoos, and went well with totally indecent gray sweatpants. Curse? What curse?

He tilted his head, roving his gaze over her as he closed the distance with a long-legged stride. His eyes heated. She could smell his spice, and her mind fogged.

"Um. Hi." Then she winced and mouthed, "Sorry. You're on the phone." As if he didn't know that already.

"I'm on hold," he said, stuffing his free hand in the pocket of his sweats. No Rolex graced his wrist today. "This is a surprise."

"Yes!" *Tone it down a notch.* "I just came by to say thank you for helping get me out of prison."

"Jail."

"Yes. Well. Thank you. Bake this at three fifty. Everything is already cooked, so it only needs to warm. Half an hour, maybe. Forty-five minutes if you want it bubbling. Don't add anymore butter, though, or you'll ruin it." She pressed the dish into his stomach, forcing him to grab it or let it drop. "Okay. Bye."

A slightly younger guy moved to the agent's side. Conrad had so filled her vision she never even realized someone else accompanied him to the lobby. The two were roughly the same height, but the similarities ended there. The new guy had hazel eyes and hair streaked by the sun.

"Hello," he said, peering at Jane with a wide grin.

Conrad kept his lips set in a firm line. For the second time since she'd met the agent, he didn't appear comfortable.

Hazel Eyes waved at her. "You must be Jane. The lady friend."

She almost curtseyed but stopped herself in time. "Yes. That's me. I mean, I'm she. Lady Jane. Or a lady named Jane. Jane Ladling."

Hold up. She'd never met this man, yet he'd recognized her on sight. Giddy excitement fluttered through her, superseding her nervousness. What had Conrad told him?

New Guy smiled with pure delight and shouldered Conrad aside to get a closer look at her. "Nice to meet you. I'm Wyatt. Con's brother. Please say you'll come up with us. He'll be busy making some calls—" he elbowed "Con"—"but I'd love the company." He angled his head toward the bank of elevators. "Shall we?"

Brother? Her lips turned up in a smile of her own. Other than a few comments here and there, Conrad had remained tight-lipped about his brother. That these two looked nothing alike meant, what?

She glanced at Conrad, silently asking, *Do I go? Do I stay?*

He conveyed no emotion as he motioned to the elevator. "After you."

Her knees knocked as she walked over and pressed the proper button. A new ding sounded, the doors opening right away. No waiting at all. Almost as if she were supposed to be here, meeting a member of Conrad's family for the first time.

Breathe. Was she ready for this?

Out of respect for his paused call, no one spoke during the ride up. Or the quick journey down the hall and past the front door, led by both boys. A little flustered, she looked around. The same parquet hardwood floors stretched across the length of the condo. Large, panoramic windows offered a gorgeous view of the city. Twelve-foot ceilings added to the urban feel. Not to mention the modern, stainless-steel appliances and the glass tile backsplash certain to be the envy of every decorator. A tufted chesterfield sofa in a light, dove gray and matching armchair angled toward the biggest LED screen she'd ever seen. Two bar stools perched beneath the long peninsula that separated the kitchen from the living room.

The place made her think Conrad had picked each piece of furniture directly off a showroom floor and had it delivered, then never used any of it. Nothing like the cozy warmth of the cottage.

Which style did he prefer?

"I didn't mean to interrupt a family get-together," she said, glancing at Conrad as he passed her, soon disappearing through a door. To store the casserole, or escape her? "I can go. I *should* go. Yes, I'll go." She fidgeted in place, feeling like she was seconds away from breaking out in a full-on sweat. "Am I saying *go* too much?"

Wyatt seemed to fight a laugh. "I ambushed him with some trouble yesterday, that's all."

"Trouble with the law?" She winced for him. "Been there."

The laugh broke free. "Yeah. I've heard about your vigilante ways. But my trouble is worse. It comes from a former foster mother."

Um, had he called her a *vigilante*?

Eager, he led her to the couch. Once she'd selected a spot in the middle, he sat on the coffee table directly in front of her, rested his forearms on his thighs and looked her over more thoroughly. "Why aren't you wearing a hat?"

"Oh. Well. I couldn't find one that complimented my dress. But, um, what have you heard about my hats?"

"Only everything. Twice." He hiked his thumb at the large screen that dominated an entire wall. "You want to watch the game over beers?" Before she could respond, he hollered, "Bro. She wants a beer. You might as well bring me a bottle, too."

"You're currently in time out. You get nothing," Conrad called. "And don't you dare ask her if she's—yes, I'm here." He said more, but the words were muffled.

Eek! What wasn't Wyatt supposed to ask her?

He rolled his eyes. "Don't let his grumpiness fool you. He adores me."

Yes, she believed that 100 percent. "You're so at ease with each other." Nothing like Jane and her siblings. Some she'd only met once. Others she'd seen a grand total of four times. "You're making me wish I'd gotten to spend more time with my brothers and sisters growing up."

He listened intently, as if dissecting each word as it escaped. "Con and I spent a couple years in the same foster facility. A place for *troubled* boys." He used air quotes. Though his tone said *no big deal*, his dark eyes told a different story. "We kinda took care of each other back then. We still do, I guess." He smiled, sheepish, but sobered fast. "He's had a rough life, and he deserves only good things."

There was a warning in his expression. And perhaps a plea.

Her heart squeezed as she imagined Conrad moving from home to home, forced to start over again and again. Jane, at least, had some constants. The adoration of her grandparents and Fiona. The Garden. Centuries-long traditions.

"I know he deserves good things," she offered quietly. Only, she could not be part of those good things long term. But how could she explain the Ladling Curse to him and make him understand? In the end, she wouldn't be the one to do the hurting—Conrad would. The moment she fell head over heels for him...Bam! Disaster. He'd be off faster than a hot knife through butter.

Doomed.

"So," Wyatt said, as if sensing the direction of her thoughts. "Are you in love with Conrad or not?"

What the—What? She cleared her throat. Better to be honest with him and manage expectations. "Oh. Um. Romantically speaking, my heart is a cold, hard machine filled with wires. And, well, we barely know each other. I mean, we know each other. But we also don't know each other."

Conrad's brother laced his fingers behind his head and leaned back slightly, acting as if he reclined in a chair. "That doesn't answer my question."

Hmm. Wyatt certainly knew how to reach the marrow of the matter. She cut a glance toward the room where Conrad had taken his call. No sign of him.

With zero help coming from the missing agent, Jane went on the offensive. "Why would you think I'm in love with him?"

"Three reasons." Wyatt raised a hand and extended one finger, then the other, saying, "That dress, and the casserole."

Jane squirmed in her seat. Was she that obvious? And no, that was not an admission. "This is an apology dress, nothing more. And yes, that's a thing. No need to look it up," she said, attempting to sound cool and casual. "So what's the third reason? You only mentioned two."

He shrugged. "Every woman falls for him."

"Every woman?" Her spine stiffened. How many had loved and lost Conrad? *Am I about to join their number?* She'd worried him again. Forced him to use his credentials to bust her free of the slammer. Visited without an invitation.

"Right?" Wyatt spread his arms, oblivious to her growing panic. "Especially when *I'm* nearby."

Conrad returned to the living room only seconds later, and her hands curled into fists. He paused when he spotted her on the couch and did a double take.

"Why are you glaring at me like that?" he asked with a wrinkled brow.

"No reason." She rose to her feet. This whole day had been a mistake. The curse was really showing off—ruining everything before anything had a chance to truly begin.

"Why are you leaving? You just got here," he said, chasing after her to the door.

She reached for the handle, ready to escape, but he caught up to her and with his chest pressed against her back, he covered her hand with his. The warmth of his touch jolted her.

"Jane," he prompted.

"I should go." After today's awkwardness, she owed herself a nice long soak in the tub and a two-hour cuddle session with Rolex. "I'd only come to drop off the casserole and say thank you for springing me from prison." Grandma Lily always said gratitude was best expressed with food.

"Jail," he corrected once again. "You sure you came for no other reason?"

He sounded as if he knew a secret she didn't. Thankful he couldn't see her face, she hurried to think of another excuse, just in case. "Yes. I, uh, came to remind you about our dinner with Tiffany and Jake. It's tomorrow. In case you'd forgotten."

He chuckled, a rumbly sound from deep in his chest that made her toes curl in her shoes. When a round of shivers kicked off, rocking her against him, she turned the door-knob, ready to bolt again. But he held her hand steady, his warm breath fanning her nape.

"Forget an evening I have been greatly anticipating?" His voice was low and husky. "No."

She relaxed her grip on the knob, then turned to face him, remaining within the circle of his arms. "Did you say *greatly anticipating*?" *And mean it?* He wasn't dreading being trapped inside a strange home with two strangers, one or both of whom might be a murderer? He looked forward to spending more time with her?

He gave her that ridiculously charming lopsided grin. "This will be our first official date, sweetheart. But more importantly, you have reminded me on four separate occasions, which is defined as pleading in my Jane 101 handbook. So yes, I said greatly anticipating."

First official date. The words echoed in her head. A double. With suspects. While working a case together. Because he wasn't done with her. The relationship wasn't ending—it was starting.

Gah! Now she panicked for another reason. *Breathe, Jay Bird.* "You should probably tell me something awful about yourself now."

"Yeah?" He looked ready to grin. "Let's see. I enjoy camping. When I take you, and I will, there will be no glamping. We will rough it and survive off the land. You will be miserable." Arching a brow, he asked, "Better?"

Deep breath in. Out. Okay. "Yes. Thank you." Although, he'd probably chop wood shirtless, ruining her distaste for camping. "D-did you do a background check on Jake Stephenson?" Better to talk about the case right now. Yes. Much better. "Any inside information you can share with the rest of the class?"

"Make her stay forever, Conrad," Wyatt called. "Did you taste this casserole?"

"Stop eating it," Conrad called back, clearly exasperated. "I just put that in the oven."

"Seriously dude. Forever. This stuff is better than crack. Not that I know what crack tastes like."

Jane swallowed a laugh. She kind of liked the uncomfortably blunt Wyatt.

Conrad toyed with a lock of her hair, saying, "Yes, I did a background check on Jacob Stephenson. During his freshman year of college, the student-run Honor Committee accused him of cheating on an exam. He was kicked out before winter break. No undergrad in the school's history had ever been sent home that quickly."

She blinked up at him. Well now. "That's good to know."

"Now that I've baited you with my hook, why don't you come inside and stay a while?" He sounded amused. "I'll let you ask me three highly personal questions."

Baited hook indeed. This man must be a killer in the interrogation room—offering what you wanted most, so you'd cave to his will. This was a deal too amazing to pass up.

She allowed him to link their fingers and lead her into the living room, where Wyatt patted the couch seat beside him. A smear of creamed pepper sauce marred his shirt now.

"Plenty of room here," he said.

Conrad released her hand to flatten his palm on the small of her back while making a low, growling sound. "You'll be taking a walk around the block while I speak with Jane."

With a heavy sigh, Wyatt unfolded to a stand. "You suck sometimes, bro."

"I know." The agent made a sweeping gesture, encompassing the entire living area. "Sit anywhere you want, sweetheart."

"So nice meeting you, Janie." Wyatt wrapped her in a hug and whispered, "Con's never called another woman sweetheart, by the way." He kissed her cheek and shot off for the door.

Her cheeks flushed. He hadn't? *It doesn't matter. It doesn't! I won't fall for him. I won't!*

Determined to enjoy the moment, Jane sank onto the middle couch cushion again. Her official spot now.

"All right." Conrad sat on the coffee table, like Wyatt. Only, he sat closer, his legs bracketing hers. "You go first. Tell me what you learned at Ana's. Who are your current main suspects now?"

Easy. "They haven't changed, really. The Kirklands, who are literal gold diggers. Robby Waynes, who is an all-around terrible person. Tiffany Hotchkins, who keeps texting me. Jake Stephenson because who is this guy, anyway? And Tony Miller, who is a thousand percent petty enough to frame me and participate in my defense." Not to mention every other man on the board of photos.

As she'd languished in double solitary confinement with Fiona yesterday—for four hours!—she'd matched photos to names and nicknames from the list of sixteen. Her memory had served her well. More than ever, she was certain something connected the guys in the images to the speed daters.

"Are Tiffany's texts bothersome?" Conrad asked, looking seconds away from a second chuckle.

"Yes! She suddenly wants to be my best friend. Why would she do that unless she hopes to pump me for information?"

"Maybe because you are a wonderful person. With the whole town gossiping about her, she might need a friend. Just a guess off the top of my head."

Jane scrunched up her nose. "No, that can't be right. Face it, Conrad. I'm known as that weird cemetery girl for a reason."

"What even is normal?" he asked. As her eyes went wide, his chuckle escaped. "So what did you find at Ana's?"

He listened, remaining still as she explained. Rather than question her further when she finished, he returned to a previous topic. "Why don't we make the three questions you get to ask me about the case?"

Why the change? And why give him time to decide not to answer anything? "Did the GBH find a person of interest who is familiar with thorn apple?"

156

"Not until yesterday. I've been scouring posts on the Headliner in my spare time. A woman discovered a bushel of the stuff growing in her neighbor's backyard."

Fiona, Team Truth's official Headliner intel collector, must have missed it, being as she'd been wrongly incarcerated for a crime she had, in fact, committed and all.

"Since the death of Miss Irons, everyone in town is on the lookout for jimsonweed," he continued. "The woman didn't identify herself or her neighbor, but I was able to track down the homeowner—Robby Waynes."

Of course! "Factor in his association with Ana, their battle over stolen money, and his awful personality, and we've got ourselves a murderer." Jane scrambled in her seat. "I should—"

"Nope. Hightower's got it covered. She's finished her preliminary research, and she's arranged an interview with him tomorrow."

Finally! Actual evidence. Details clicking into place. "Robby probably robbed Blake and accused Ana of the crime. Ana went digging and discovered hard proof to send Robby to prison. Worked into a panic, Robby then poisoned Ana's morning beverage and entrapped me to remove me from the cemetery and get his hands on my nonexistent gold."

"Or maybe he, too, is being framed? Finding the jimsonweed was too easy."

Ugh! Jane vacillated between the excitement of taking down someone so awful and uncertainty.

Was she really going to talk herself into *not* suspecting Robby? "Who else could it be?"

"I've got my eye on Blake Crawford. Miss Irons referenced a man named B-rye in her journal. Supposedly, he impersonated four other men in order to empty their bank accounts."

Okay, this was beyond interesting. "When did you learn this?"

"Yesterday when I spoke with Hightower. She mentioned a man Ana speculated stole this B-rye's identity in order to drain *his* accounts. The Robber."

A revenge theft? "I *knew* Robby was the Robber!"

Except, total confusion quickly set in. "Let me get this straight. Ana believed Robby stole from Blake and that Blake stole from Robby, as well as four others."

"Correct. There were twenty-three other names. Each guy was thought to have stolen from someone else on the list, but we've discovered no real connections between the individuals. Well, other than they were all males."

Wow. So many other names to explore and cross reference. Her workload basically exploded.

Jane squared her shoulders. *I've got this. I'm a caretaker of the dead, and I can handle whatever comes my way.*

"You've asked your three questions, but I'm a giver, so I'll give you a fourth," Conrad said, threading his fingers through hers once again. He grazed his thumb over her now-racing pulse. "A bonus."

Never one to refuse a gift, she peered into his eyes and asked what she suddenly wanted to know more than anything else in the world. "Am I invited to dinner? I hear the casserole is utterly divine."

CHAPTER THIRTEEN

"A dollop of sugar for two!"
Sweet Lips, Tennessee - Sweet Success Shindig
10 Matches Made!

The morning of the dinner and Robby's interview with Agent Hightower dawned at last. Jane woke with a smile, her limbs tangled in soft sheets and Rolex curled into her side. The sun hadn't yet dawned, but her eyes easily adjusted to the darkness in her bedroom and the mess she'd caused last night.

After dinner with Conrad, she'd come home to search for the perfect first date dress and hat to wear to Tiffany's. Though she'd tried on everything she owned, nothing had struck her as good enough. Looked like she'd be forced to spend the day shopping rather than investigating.

Jane swiped up her phone and padded to the kitchen with her fur-child in tow. She prepared Rolex's breakfast, as well as a pot of coffee, then poured herself a mug and settled in at the round kitchen table to read any messages. There were five.

A-hole Miller: *Update me on our case.*

Mrs. Hots: *So excited to see you tonight! 7 pm sharp*

Mrs. Hots: *I forgot to ask if you have any dietary restrictions??? Let me know ASAP so I can inform the chef. Prepare to be dazzled!!!!!!*

Mrs. Hots: *Oh!!! We should probably coordinate our costumes, yes? I'd hate to wear the same thing.*

Mrs. Hots: *Lolololololol I forgot to tell you this is a themed dinner, didn't I? Well, now you know. I selected Fated Mates. :) :) :) How cute is that?!*

A theme? Fated mates? "This is going to be a challenge—for Conrad," she told Rolex as he jumped onto the table and settled in the empty centerpiece bowl. Would her oh-so-serious boyfriend agree to dress up?

Rolex yawned at her.

"What am I supposed to even suggest to him?" Jane asked. "A doctor and patient? They're kind of fated, right? Or is that too reminiscent of the last case?"

The world's most perfect feline licked his hindquarters.

"Yeah, you're right," Jane said with a nod. "The last thing Tiffany wants is a reminder of her dead, cheating husband. Okay, what about a book nerd and a book boyfriend? Not that a woman who loves books is automatically a nerd. More like a goddess, amiright?" She herself had an especially delightful collection of romances and mysteries.

Rolex stretched, clearly not wowed by her newest suggestion.

She snapped her fingers. "I've got it. We can go as characters from a heartwarming Christmas movie. The cookie baker and the real estate developer. The hometown star athlete who returns home and the ex-girlfriend who's losing her father's candle shop. They're all fated mates, right, so—"

Blink. Rolex-speak for *get serious.*

Okay, moving on. "Why don't we go as Pops and

Grandma Lily? I can dress in a gold lame halter top and Conrad can wear a belted cable-knit sweater. Although in this heat, he'll pass out before the second course is served." Though she supposed she *could* nurse him back to health...

She shook her head, and an idea struck. Grabbing her phone, she typed her response to Tiffany: *Very excited. No dietary restrictions. Thank you for the information. Does salt and pepper count as fated mates? See you soon.*

Surely Conrad would have no problem attending as a condiment. He could wear all black, and Jane could wear all white. Problem solved.

She ignored Tony and sent a message to Conrad: *Just found out there's a theme tonight. A THEME!!! Don't worry, I've come up with the perfect solution. You're gonna love it.*

The more she typed, the more intense her excitement became. Conrad dressed up, even the slightest bit... *Yes, please.*

Agent Spice: *Call Tiffany and cancel.*

Oh, no, no, no. As his "sweetheart," Jane deserved certain privileges.

Jane: *But it's Fated Mates, Conrad. FATED MATES!!!! Sounds fun.*

Agent Spice: *Cancel.*

Jane: *Think of it as role playing. Did I mention you're gonna love my idea? I'll give you a hint—you're gonna be a little spicy and I'm gonna be a little salty.*

Agent Spice: *Really. Cancel.*

Jane: *Aren't you eager to spend an evening with me??? But okay, fine. I guess I can ask Beau to accompany me instead. And yes, this is me manipulating you, bending you to my will. Beau and I will look amazing as a superhero and his unobtainable crush, don't you think?*

Agent Spice: *I'll pick you up at 7.*

Her heart leapt. *In costume?*

Agent Spice: *Yes. I've got it handled.*

Jane: *As a superhero???? Stop being mysterious, Officer Detective Special Agent Ryan. We've got to match, remember?*

Agent Spice: *I'll be a hardened detective, and you'll be my most elusive case. I'll need to study you in great detail.*

Wheezing her next breath, she fanned her cheeks. What was this guy doing to her?

Jane: *I think I can manage that.*

In fact, no shopping was needed. She already had the perfect outfit. Instead of an "elusive case," she'd go as an ace reporter willing to leave no gravestone unturned—*thank you, Conrad*—to find all the clues and help the big bad detective solve the case.

When her stomach ceased fluttering, she texted Beau to remind him of the promise he hadn't yet given to babysit Rolex and watch for those plotting, thieving Waynes.

Beaudyguard: *I'll be there, and I'll bring my friends.*

They'd arrived in town? Oh, how wonderful. First, she'd met Conrad's brother. Now she'd get to interact with Beau's military pals. The more the merrier. But that reminded her. This whole mess started because she'd wanted to set Beau up with a nice girl. While one of those girls had died, another was still out there. Why hadn't Eunice Parks ever returned Jane's calls?

Perhaps a visit was in order?

After washing up and completing the morning rounds, Jane (finally) typed up the sixteen nicknames with known identities, along with the list of attendants from Digging for Gold, then clicked her mouse to print. She added the photos of Ana's purse contents to the queue. Then Tiffany and Jake's selfie. As the ancient machine chugged along, slapping ink line by line, Jane recreated the journalist's colorful sticky notes that detailed the crimes she'd posted on the Headliner.

Once all the pages finished printing, she spread everything on the kitchen counter. With a flick of her wrist, she opened *Truth Be Told*. Time to refine her thoughts, suspicions, suspects and plans, so she would know what to (stealthily) ask Tiffany and Jake tonight—while also preparing a meal for Beau and friends as a thank you. Chicken and dumplings should do the trick. And a few sides. No more than half a dozen, probably. And maybe a pan of banana pudding. Also bread pudding in case anyone hated bananas. Probably a whiskey and butter cake too.

Rolex stalked across the counter again and again, making sure to sit on a new picture or paper with each relocation. All the while, Jane alternated between baking and studying. Stir batter. Tape theory notes to the large rolling white board she borrowed from the office. Chop vegetables. Stretch lines of colored yarn between note cards or pictures to connect suspects with evidence or even one another. Each color represented a different speculation.

Though she nixed the shovel key and mini hammer, the bagged panties made the board. Conrad believed Ana had carried them for overnight surveillance, but Jane wasn't convinced. What if Ana had been seeing someone? A re-try with Robby... a fling with Blake... or perhaps someone else. And what about Jake, who she'd encountered at Digging for Gold?

Robby. Blake. Jake. Something about the photos of those particular guys drew Jane's gaze, one after the other. What was she missing? What was that niggle in the back of her brain?

She didn't mean to, but she worked through lunch. Plus her first snack. And the second. Also the third. When she ultimately pulled herself from the sleuthing spiral, she realized she only had an hour to prepare for her date. Worse, she almost burned her fried green tomatoes.

After storing the food in carriers that doubled as plate

warmers, she rushed through a shower, dried her hair, and applied a bit of makeup. Rolex watched from the bed as she donned a dark gray pencil skirt every hard-hitting female reporter wore in the comics. And, because she took dressing up seriously, she added a zebra-striped top with a kitty-cat bow. Luckily, she had the perfect black fedora hat. She printed the word "Press" on flowery cardstock and tucked it into the hat's band.

A knock sounded at her front door. A hard double rap. Conrad! He'd beaten Beau here.

Butterflies took flight in her stomach. "Behave," she told Rolex, rushing to the entrance. Only it wasn't Conrad on the other side but Beau with his three friends, all big, all muscly, all giving her a once over as if she were on display at a zoo. Muted sunlight framed them.

Might as well get into character. "The name's Solva. Solva Case from the Headliner. Tell me your biggest secrets, boys," Jane said with a wink.

Beau looked her over and grinned. "You are...wow."

Wow was good, right?

"Hate to interrupt, but what's that I'm smelling?" one of the friends asked. He closed his eyes and groaned. "Is it Heaven? I'm smelling Heaven, aren't I?"

Beau cleared his throat and scrubbed a hand through his hair, disheveled and sheepish. "Apologies for the knock. I just wanted to see—never mind. We are reporting for duty, boss. Jane, meet Trick, Isaac and Holden."

"Welcome, welcome. I don't know what Beau has told you about my hourly rates, but I pay in pennies, dinner, and dessert. I whipped up a little something if you guys are hungry." Jane sure hoped there was enough chicken and dumplings in the 12-quart pot. Good thing she'd added the three cheese potatoes, garlic green beans, those fried green tomatoes, as well as fried squash medallions, yam casserole, homemade rolls, the two puddings, the whiskey cake and peach cobbler. "Feel free to help yourself to anything in the kitchen."

She stepped aside. The men filed into the living room, each nodding and mumbling, "Ma'am," as they passed. And oh good gracious, the foursome took up a lot of space. They all exuded the same high intensity.

Rolex allowed Beau to pass without hissing. His friends did not receive the same courtesy. To her immense relief, no member of the trio seemed perturbed by the ferocious feline.

"Jane," Beau said. "The door."

Right. She should close it. She turned—whoa! There Conrad stood, holding the loveliest funeral arrangement she'd ever seen, with white carnations, creamy pink chrysanthemums and delicate peach roses. The stomach fluttering started up all over again. The heart racing too.

He offered her the flowers, and she accepted, hugging the blooms to her chest. Her first bouquet.

"Thank you," she said, batting her lashes at him. "I love them so much."

He wore a dark suit, as usual, but he'd added a vest and polished antique cufflinks, giving him a vintage vibe. Perfect in any era. Dashing. Sophisticated. *Devastating.*

"We'll be in the kitchen, stuffing our faces," Beau said behind her.

Jane's attention remained locked on her date as footsteps flared and faded. She waggled her brows at Conrad. "You said hardened detective, *not* the world's sexiest bachelor detective."

"I thought that was a given," he deadpanned. His dark gaze slid over her slowly, heating, and her stomach dipped. "You are the world's most beautiful reporter, determined to write a story on me and get straight to the heart of the matter."

His words seemed to suggest a thousand things at once, and she struggled to catch her breath. "Let's put these in water before we go." She led him to the kitchen, leaving the guys to introduce themselves.

She gave the blooms another hug before placing the stems in Grandma Lily's favorite crystal vase.

Manage your expectations, Jay Bird. Deep breath in, out. This was a first date, yes, but also a night undercover. Two people who sometimes imagined kissing each other, secretly interrogating a widow and her new boyfriend, while having fun in the process. It didn't have to be a huge deal.

Head high, Jane faced her guests. Everyone spoke comfortably in relaxed postures and tossed back the fried medallions as if they were candy.

Conrad winked at her, and a white-hot flush spread over her skin. "You ready?"

"I am." She kissed Rolex, patted Beau's cheek, and waved to his friends before linking arms with Conrad and heading to his sedan.

Cool night air fragrant with magnolias enveloped them. The muted sunlight offered only the slightest glow. Honestly, with the carpets of soft green grass, flower patches thriving and trees swaying in a gentle breeze, Jane felt as if she'd stumbled into a dream.

He opened the passenger door and even held her elbow as she eased into the seat none too gracefully.

"These pencil skirts are no joke," she grumbled. Much more difficult to maneuver in than her usual fit and flares.

"I promise you the skirt is worth every hardship...to me." His husky voice and heated gaze sent her heartbeat into another dizzying rush.

By the time he settled behind the wheel and drove down the road, she had almost recovered half of her good sense. The car smelled and felt like him. Spice and warmth and...

perfection. How was she supposed to recover the other half of her good sense in these conditions?

"You want to small talk or get straight to convincing me we must secretly interrogate the happy couple for a specific piece of information?" he asked.

"Yes. That." She twisted in her seat as much as the buckle would allow. "I'd like to learn about Jake's past relationships and Tiffany's financial state." A need for money might point to the need to work with the Waynes to hunt for gold. "Oh, and if either of them likes to garden."

"Most people don't host dinner parties and invite an agent of the law if they've committed murder," he pointed out.

"But some people do," she replied without missing a beat. "I would. And for all we know, Tiffany and Jake hope to interrogate *us*. Oh! Speaking of possible murderers, what happened during Hightower's interview with Robby? Did she learn anything?"

"He wasn't arrested, but he wasn't cleared either. Hightower is double-checking several of his statements, including the one about *not* meeting with Miss Irons the morning she died. There is a witness who put them together, claiming they spoke earlier that morning."

"Who?"

"Hightower wouldn't tell me because she knew I'd tell you. But she did admit she's also looking into Blake Crawford. Like Fiona, she believes the man is innocent. Honestly, so do I."

"Yeah. I do, too." Jane bit her bottom lip. She'd crossed someone off her list at last, yet the remaining possibilities seemed endless. Suspects loomed everywhere.

The drive ended a few too-brief minutes later when he parked in the Hotchkins's driveway, next to Jake's polished-until-it-glistened black sports car. Again, Conrad opened the passenger door for her, then extended a hand to aid her emergence from the car. Instead of dropping her hand once she stood solidly on both legs, he twined his fingers through hers and held on.

Jane got *more* fluttery. They strolled to the porch, their sides brushing together. He rang the bell, and she glanced back at his sedan. Suddenly the urge to rush somewhere else, anywhere else, nearly overpowered her. Just so they could be alone instead of spending the evening with other people.

Tiffany and Jake answered the door only a few seconds later—together. They, too, held hands. He wore a tux; she wore a flowing white gown with endless layers of tulle. Jane's eyes widened. They'd dressed as a groom and his very sexy bride. The skirt had a slit that almost reached her hip and a bodice so low, she was afraid two more guests were soon to pop out and attend the party. So different from Tiffany's understated attire as a doctor's wife.

They were both all smiles until the widow eyed Conrad up and down. She propped her hands on her hips, her lips in a faux pout. "Did Jane forget to tell you this was a costume party?"

"He's in costume." An idea hit Jane, and she decided to launch an experiment. Hopefully, Conrad would roll with it. "He's a killer pretending to be a detective, and I'm the local journalist who is figuring out all his secrets. A match made in...well, somewhere." She glanced between Tiffany and Jake, judging their reaction to her words.

Tiffany appeared dismayed, while Jake conveyed confusion.

Hmm. Results of experiment: inconclusive. Either their responses were genuine and totally normal or fake and pointing to guilt.

The widow Hotchkins recovered quickly. "Welcome.

Please, come in." She and Jake eased back. Still holding hands.

Conrad ushered Jane inside, her high heels tapping on the black-and-white marble flooring in the foyer. Like the last time she'd visited, Tiffany guided the way through the home. This time she smiled, pointing out the paintings Jake had created just for her, confirming Jane's suspicions that Jake was Art Amour. The widow offered minor details, like how he'd chosen a particular color palette because her lipstick inspired him.

They passed the vast sitting room where Jane had once stood awkwardly among a sea of mourning women after the not-so-good doctor's demise. Any trace of the dearly departed was gone. Every picture. All mementos. Not a hint that he'd ever even existed. Now paintings by Tiffany's soon-to-be new husband covered the walls.

And still the merry widow led on, giving a full-on tour. Jane relied on Conrad to guide her forward as she rubber-necked, studying the eclectic array of canvases. She'd never been an appreciator of what others considered "fine art." She liked what she liked. These paintings of Jake's...

They were elaborate and fancy, some lovely, some not so amazing to her tastes. One stood out to her more than any other. In it, he'd combined the water lilies of a Monet with the stars in Van Gogh's *Starry Night*. A bold statement summed up her knowledge of art. Had he drawn inspiration from the "greats," or was he some kind of forger? The secret Ana discovered, perhaps? Was that why he had the star by his name? Grr. The journalist might not have suspected Jake of being the speed dating bandit at all.

The tour concluded in the formal dining room. Ah. There were the world's most uncomfortable Queen Anne chairs. The long table, suitable for seating at least twenty people, had four elaborate place settings ready to go. A butler stood nearby with a tray of fizzing champagne flutes.

"Have you ever tasted a peach julep?" Tiffany asked, passing out glasses. "They are to die for."

To die for. *Is she mocking me now?* And alcohol? Tonight? She should keep her wits and refuse. But even still, she accepted a glass, for the sake of appearances.

"To fresh starts," Tiffany toasted.

"To fresh starts," Jane echoed, raising her glass. She took a sip, just a sip. Oh, wow. What a delicious treat. Surely a little alcohol wouldn't be amiss. She drained half the glass. But only half...of the second glass, because she'd already finished the first.

Their group continued to stand, chatting about nothing important, sipping more of that delectable peach julep. Conrad remained at ease, holding but not drinking the julep. He was articulate and well mannered, charming as easily as breathing, making her repeatedly forget her purpose. Every time she remembered, however, she wanted to shake him. He kept the conversation light, never creating an opening for a single leading question.

Eventually, Tiffany and Jake got lost in a private exchange.

"If you'd like any help tonight," Conrad whispered, his lips hovering over the shell of Jane's ear, "you've got to stop distracting me."

Goose bumps double parked on her skin. "I'm only standing here. How is that distracting?" Then she spotted the twinkle in Conrad's whiskey eyes, and she forgot her train of thought.

"Oh! You two are almost as cute as we are," Tiffany said laughingly as Jake planted kisses along the side of her face.

Either they were really in love or excellent actors.

"So," Tiffany said, finishing off her own julep. "How's the

case coming?" Innocent question—or sly? "Have you found the killer yet?"

Okay, so, they could be both in love and excellent actors. Had *their* interrogation just begun?

Jane squared her shoulders and gave a hopeful, almost imperceptible nod to Conrad. *Go on. There's your opening.*

He knew how to communicate with his eyes, too. *This is your show, sweetheart.*

Very well. "Not yet," she piped up, "but there are several persons of interest."

"We'll get our man," Conrad said with a practiced smile. "Or woman."

"We always do." Without barely a breath, she asked her own leading question. "You knew Ana, didn't you, Jake?"

Tiffany stiffened ever so slightly. Oh, oh, oh. From jealousy?

"Briefly." His perma-grin turned sad. "We attended a few events together, but we were never a perfect match. She had her eyes on another attendee. Robby...something."

Old news.

"Ana was found on your property, wasn't she, Jane?" Tiffany swiped another glass of deliciousness for herself, taking a huge swallow.

"She was, yes." What was the widow getting at? "I'm told she was working on several stories about scandalous things happening in town."

The liquid in Tiffany's glass rippled. *She's shaking.* Afraid of a specific story? "I've heard the same, and I fear the turmoil those rumors are going to cause the town." The brunette pressed a hand against her heart, as though moved by the topic. "I'm sure you heard about Robby and Ana's fight the morning she died."

Jane perked up. "I did, yes."

"I hated telling Agent Hightower what I observed. Robby

is a sweetheart. He might have a temper, but he'd never murder a girl."

Wait. *Tiffany* was the witness? Did that mean she'd seen what she claimed to see...or that she'd lied to cover her own crime? "So much wild speculation is flying about the big, bad fight." Truth. Courtesy of Jane herself. "I'd love to hear a firsthand account."

As if the widow had hoped for just such an invitation, she leaned toward Jane to say, "Robby moved in with Abigail a few weeks ago. She and I decided to enjoy a day of pampering. Shopping, mani-pedis, facials. The works. At the salon, I stepped out to answer a phone call from Jake. Robby was there. I mean, I didn't see his face, but I caught his backside as he was walking away from Ana, flipping her the bird. She was leaning out of the window of her car to insult his mother."

"I remember that," Jake said with his customary smile. "You accidentally hung up on me. I was so worried about you."

"What happened next?" Jane asked, trying to decide if the story was rehearsed.

Tiffany hiked her shoulders in a shrug. "Nothing. Robby ran off, and Ana peeled out."

Jake set his empty glass aside. "Does Robby continue to deny the encounter?"

The widow nodded. "Yes, but that is understandable. The encounter makes him look guilty, even though he's innocent."

Was he innocent? What happened before Tiffany broke up the pair? The poisoning of Ana's coffee? "You're sure it was Robby you saw? You got a good look at him?" As much as Jane liked blaming Robby, she had to wonder... What if the real thief dressed up as Robby to frame him?

"Oh yes." Another nod from Tiffany. "He was wearing his

favorite ball cap and sunglasses. Anyway. Enough about that. Let's focus on positive things tonight. Like love." She brightened. "Why don't we take a photo to commemorate this night?"

Jane wanted to protest the subject change. She was still torn. If the thief wasn't Robby, but someone pretending to be him, the thief wasn't Jake, who'd been on the phone at the time. Unless it was Jake. Somehow. Argh!

"What you want, you get." The man in question winked at his fiancée, then withdrew a cell phone from his jacket pocket. "I'm happy to take the photo, babe."

"Babe." The other woman stomped her foot, zooming into bridezilla mode. "You know I like you to be in the photos with me."

"All right, all right." He laughed, lifting the cell as everyone squeezed together. "One. Two." He kissed Tiffany's cheek and snapped the shot. "Three."

Darn! Jane had probably shut her eyes.

"I'll be sure to tag you when I post, Jane," Tiffany said.

"I don't have a social media account." Though she should get one, probably. For the Garden. "I'd love a copy texted to me, though. Right away." And Jake's phone number. Beau might be able to gather intel with it. Like where he'd been when he made that fateful call. She rattled off her contact information. "That way, you won't forget."

Jake shrugged. "No problem."

Her phone dinged only seconds later. And yes, she'd closed her eyes. Conrad hadn't kissed her cheek, like boyfriends tended to do apparently, but he *had* peered directly at her for the photo and oh, was that far better. And much worse. He looked as if he'd found what he wanted more than his next breath.

He *couldn't* want her that much. No one could. He must be acting for the sake of their companions. Yes, yes. Acting.

"How do I look?" he asked, rubbing his stubbled jawline.

"Like a tasty snack," she blurted truthfully. Her eyes widened as soon as the words registered. Hmm, maybe he would think *she* acted too.

"A snack, hmm," he replied, his irises alight with humor. "Tell me more."

Danged peach julep!

The butler rang a bell to signal the arrival of the first course. The best time to launch a search-and-see.

"May I use your restroom?" Jane asked. "To wash my hands before we eat."

"Of course. I'll show you where it is," the other woman offered.

Oh. Well. The next best thing, she supposed. Alone time with Tiff.

"Miss me," Tiffany said, kissing Jake's cheek.

He smiled at her as if she had hung the moon. "Don't stay away too long. My heart won't survive."

"Jane." Exasperation and dread filled Conrad's tone. His irises blazed. *Do nothing you shouldn't.* "Don't forget, sweetheart. Killers like to hunt their prey. Come back to me quickly, or I will go hunting." His warning was clear, but his husky voice sent a thrill down her spine.

"I'll think about maybe considering possibly missing you." Jane had no idea why she did what she next did—no, not true. She had an inkling. The peach julep. High on bubbly, she pressed a soft, lingering kiss into his lips.

When she met his gaze, his eyes blazed with another message. One she wasn't ready to decipher.

"This way," she muttered, showing Tiffany the path out of her own dining room.

"Slow down," the hostess said with a little laugh. Then she never stopped talking, relaying wedding planning highlights. The stories—never—ended. How Jake agreed with her color scheme, how he loved her choice of flowers, and how he trusted her vision, blah, blah, blah.

Was Jake too good to be true? Sure sounded like it. If Jane were to plan a wedding with Conrad—not that she would. Dang, dang, dang. *Ignore the flare of longing.* She would never ever *never* dare risk the curse, would she?

"Is Abigail Waynes-Kirkland a bridesmaid?" she interjected, needing a distraction.

"She's the maid of honor. Why? Are you upset that she got swept up by the rumor of riches buried in the cemetery and briefly considered digging up a grave? You should forgive her, Jane. She's close to bankrupt, and she's desperate, but she realized her mistake. Knows how disgusting it would be to handle a body and decided not to do it. Oh! Did I tell you about the caterer?"

Was that the truth about Abigail? A lie? A scheme of some sort? Jane wanted to ask, but she could only wash her hands for so long before things got awkward.

Upon their return, Conrad and Jake ended a discussion about the importance of shading in landscapes. Had he used the one-on-one to learn anything useful? 'Cause that sounded incredibly boring.

Jake, who'd taken his seat, smiled, jumped up, and helped Tiffany into hers. Conrad did not help Jane. Instead, he remained reclined in a pose of relaxation and arched a brow at her.

She scrunched up her lips to convey her failure.

Two waiters glided into the room to serve the first course. And. Hmm. A platter of slimy rocks?

"Baked snails in a bed of bubbling parmesan, ma'am," the server explained as he set a plate in front of her.

"My favorite," Jake said with a wider smile.

"Oh. Um." Jane tried not to wince. "Thank you?"

There was no question now; these people were absolutely

guilty of a crime—the ruination of her appetite. One fake nibble after another, Jane hid the starter in her napkin.

Might as well launch her interrogation while she pretended to eat snails. *Snails.* "Tell me about yourself, Jake," she said, stealing a bite of garnish. Something to appease her churning stomach.

"What would you like to know?" the painter asked, giving Tiffany another smile, as if they shared a silent, secret joke.

Hmm. What if the couple *wanted* her to eat the garnish? There was no other reason to serve snails. For all she knew, that garnish was a poisonous herb. The killer *did* possess knowledge about gardening and killer plants...

No, no, no. The pair wouldn't dare to off her here. Not with a special agent in the house. Still, Jane emptied her champagne flute, hoping to dilute any toxin. Wow. Did *anything* taste better than a peach julep?

"Jane." Conrad nudged her shoulder. "Did you have a question for Jake?"

Right! "Where are you from?"

Jake dropped his fork with a clatter. On purpose? His lips turned down for the first time, his whole being brimming with melancholy—which sent her internal lie detector on hyper-alert. Needles dancing, ink running off the page. All the while, Tiffany rubbed his shoulder. A gesture of comfort.

"I'm sorry," he said. "I haven't thought of home in years. The last time I was there, I buried my mother."

"That's okay, babe." Tiffany leaned over to kiss his cheek. "Everyone understands."

Jane swallowed a frustrated huff. With his words, he'd shut down any further questioning along that line. A practiced move or a genuine sentiment?

The wait staff returned to clear their plates before bringing in the second course. A single thumb sized brown cracker with chopped vegetables piled on top of it. "Corn, cucumber and radish tartines," the server told her.

"Maybe I could have extra?" she asked.

Conrad leaned over to kiss her cheek and murmur, "I'll feed you afterward."

New goose bumps spread over one side of her body.

"Speaking of extra... Babe, can I tell them?" Tiffany burst out. "I want to tell them." She grinned, clapped, and decided not to wait for her fiancé's reply. But then, he was too busy smiling again. "We're leaving for Paris on Monday. In three months, we'll return as Mr. and Mrs. Stephenson."

What? Monday. The day after Sunday. Which was tomorrow. No, no, no. No! That couldn't happen. Jane couldn't lose access to Tiffany and Jake until the conclusion of the investigation. They were prime suspects. Jake, more than ever.

His smile bothered Jane. Like, it never wavered unless you happened to mention his (allegedly) dead mother. That good mood *must* be fake. No one could be that nice, that often, without secretly killing people in their spare time.

His picture on the white board bothered her, too. And what was with Tiffany's eagerness to get out of town? Why the rush?

Okay, time to speed the investigation along. "I'm throwing a party," Jane announced.

"She isn't," Conrad said with a shake of his head.

"Oh, but I am." She rattled off details as they formed inside her head. "Come one, come all. Bring your significant other or find one. That's the motto. For the party I'm throwing. To celebrate love and also something I did. An accomplishment. Because I discovered gold on my property. Yes! Abigail was right. There were hidden nuggets waiting to be uncovered." Truth, just not literal. A piece of wisdom equaled a nugget of gold. Something Jane *had* found at the Garden.

Tiffany appeared skeptical.

So Jane continued. "I'm going to show them off. The nuggets, I mean. They're big. Huge. The theme is glitz and glamor, and I'll be auctioning off a nugget as well as a date with my friend Beau. Possibly his three friends." Her gaze darted to Conrad, who regarded her with a piercing stare that grew more intense as she revealed each new horror. "You're all invited, and I won't take no for an answer."

Now the widow flicked a quick glance toward Jake, who lifted his shoulders as if to say: *You decide, babe.*

Okay, time to cinch the deal. "Did I forget to mention this is also an engagement party? For the two of you. Because we are celebrating love, and yours is the gold star of relationships." Playing her part, Jane slapped a hand across her mouth as if she'd let something slip. "Surprise?"

Intrigue lit up Tiffany's eyes. *Yes. I've got her.*

"All right. We'll be there," the widow said. "We probably won't stay long, but we'll definitely make an appearance. You're auctioning off a nugget of gold?"

"Yes." And that wasn't a lie. Beau's heart *must* be made of gold. "Wonderful." Then Jane's phone rang. Grateful for the interruption, she dug the cell out of her pocket and held up an index finger. "This is Rolex's babysitter, so I better take it. Please feel free to talk amongst yourselves."

Slinking in her seat, she pressed the device against her ear and whispered, "Is something wrong?"

"We caught them," Beau said, triumphant. "We caught the Waynes." A shout sounded in the background, and he cursed. "Or not. Just get here."

CHAPTER FOURTEEN

"Single for the very last time!"
Lovington, New Mexico - Lovestruck Celebration!
15 Matches Made!

"They got away," Beau said, his voice flat and shoulders hunched in shame.

Jane hesitated on the cottage porch steps, Conrad at her side. Night had fallen, the world behind them covered by a thick veil of darkness. Crickets and locusts sang in the background, the perfect accompaniment to the magnolia scented breeze.

Beau and a dirt-streaked Fiona stood where Ana's body had been found, both illuminated by the bright light that spilled from the windows. Rolex watched from inside the house, splayed across the pane.

"The guys are searching the grounds," Beau continued, his hands balled, "but it's not looking good."

"What happened?" With a hand on her lower back, Conrad encouraged Jane to make the rest of the climb.

Fiona winced and raised her hand. "I might be at fault for this. But how was I supposed to know a surprise visit to leave some yarn on your porch could cause so much trouble?"

Beau massaged his temples, frustration stamped on every feature of his face. "There were three trespassers, each wearing a ski mask and carrying a shovel. They came on foot and headed straight to Autumn Grove. We let them do it. The plan was to give them enough space to set up and catch them in the act. They didn't falter, just started digging up the plot with the weeping angel."

Plot 51. It housed a coffin marked by the Order of Seven. Of course the trio had gone there.

Forgive Abigail for nearly desecrating Jane's home a second time, as Tiffany had suggested? *Over my dead bodies.* "Go on."

"The moment they unearthed their first shovelful—which we've already fixed—we swooped in. There was a chase. We corralled them."

Jane imagined the scene. Four ex-soldiers, calmly and efficiently cornering the threat.

"Then I arrived," Fiona said, wringing her hands. "The boys were so focused on protecting me, they lost the Dirty Three–the Tri-Squad? You're so good at naming the criminals, Jane, so I'll leave that up to you. Anyway. They escaped. I tried to help catch them and got tackled." The tension melted off her as a dreamy sigh slipped out. "It was pretty much a highlight of my life. That Holden is powerful, isn't he? Almost as strong as Sheriff Moore."

"The Three Maskedateers?" Jane offered. "No, that's far too friendly, considering the crime. I'll keep thinking."

"I'm sure you'll come up with something perfect." Fiona took in Jane and Conrad, standing so close, and grinned. "How was your date?"

Apprehension thrummed from Conrad. Okay then. Still not happy about that impromptu party announcement. Noted.

"Well." Jane removed her hat to busy her hands. The "Press" placard she'd tucked inside the satiny band fluttered to the porch as if to proclaim *play time's over, kids*. "I kind of promised to throw a party tomorrow night to celebrate all the gold I might have suggested I found."

"Suggested?" Conrad sputtered.

"And I may have also bragged about auctioning you off for a date, Beau. So. You know. It could have gone a *little* better."

"You did *what?*" Beau demanded.

"Don't worry," Jane told him, brushing their worries aside with a fluttery wave. "I'll invite Eunice."

"Oh, this is brilliant." Grinning, Fiona pressed a hand over her heart. "Absolutely brilliant."

Jane beamed at her. "Thank you for noticing. Unlike some people." A quick, expectant glance at Conrad. Nope. No better.

"Let's hear what you hope to accomplish with this party," he said, his voice tight.

"Our prime suspects were about to skip town for three months." Jane spread her arms. "If one is a murderer, the other should know it."

Conrad ran his tongue over his teeth. "Our?"

She looped her arm through his. "We're a team, remember? All of us. Team Truth. This shindig might not go as smoothly as last time—"

"Smoothly? You got us both drugged," Beau reminded her.

"Yes, but I also caught the killer. And I'll do it again, you watch and see. I'll bring everyone together, like before, turn up the heat, sprinkle in a little zaniness and boom! The murder is solved." Why mess with such a flawless plan? "Seems to me the girls are the only ones getting things done around here."

"I was just thinking the same thing," Fiona said with a serious nod.

"I mean, I'm *still* waiting to hear what you learned about Jake and his past girlfriends." Jane squeezed Conrad's bicep. Oh! His very well-defined bicep. "I know there were at least two."

"I called the girlfriends. One shouted an obscenity at me and hung up. The other went to voice mail. No return calls. None of which matters right now. There will be no party," Conrad insisted. "Not big, not small, not anything. No. Party."

"We should begin planning immediately," Fiona exclaimed. "Over blueberry pancakes!"

"Are you serious?" Blueberry pancakes? Today? After snails and crackers? Jane nearly whimpered with relief. "Yes!" She bounced on her feet, then all but burst through the front door like the Kool Aid Man, leading the charge inside the house.

Rolex wasn't happy when the crowd invaded his turf, especially when Beau's friends returned and bellied up to the table with everyone else to await the best meal ever to be enjoyed in the history of meals.

As Fiona whipped up her masterpiece in the kitchen, the boys discussed security measures for the party. Jane listened with half an ear, fork and knife in hand, and mind whirling. She had her suspects pared down to five names. Abigail, her ex, Robby—the Dirty Three. Yeah, that one worked. They were thieves, plain and simple. The kind of people who would steal Blake Crawford's identity and money, then kill Ana to hide their crime. Tonight's actions had proven it beyond a reasonable doubt.

There was also too eager Tiffany and too nice Jake. Cohorts in crime?

Tomorrow's celebration would allow Jane to do five things. Ply her guests with peach julep, her new favorite drink. An extra splash of bourbon or twelve might encourage loose lips. *Thanks for the idea, Tiffany and Jake.* Observe the Party of Five–Hang Five?–as they interacted with each other because yes, Jane was inviting the Waynes and yes, they would accept despite everything. How could they not? They would risk anything to get their grubby paws on her gold.

She petted Rolex, who curled up in the centerpiece as usual, while everyone plotted and planned. The guys droned on about egresses and extra cameras. They also grumbled. A lot. How could they continue to miss the beauty of this party? It provided the perfect cover to observe the five as they interacted with Blake, whom she would invite as well. He would accept when she made an offer he couldn't refuse…somehow. And bonus, she would discover who treated her differently now that she'd "found" gold. Oh, and if she masterminded a confession out of the killer, that was just gravy.

Everything was doable. Probably. It was worth a shot, at least.

"Hope you're hungry," Fiona called. "The first stack is almost ready."

"We're starved," Jane called back.

Conrad nudged her shoulder with his own. Jacketless, he appeared relaxed again, with an elbow propped on the table. His tie was open, the top buttons of his shirt undone. He'd rolled up his sleeves. One leg was bent, his ankle resting on his knee. His dark hair possessed no kind of order and all kinds of mess, as if he'd plowed a hand through it only seconds ago.

"What will it mean for our relationship if I'm not a fan of these pancakes?" he asked.

Oh, that's right. He'd never tried them. The day after she'd solved the Hots case, Conrad had come over to talk. Fiona had been in the process of making the first batch of goodness in months that had seemed like years. By the time Jane and Conrad had ended their conversation, the hotcakes were devoured, the last drop of batter scraped from the bowl.

"Let's put it this way. It's more important for you to like them over me," she teased. Maybe, probably. These pancakes were *everything.* True Heaven on Earth. A wonder of the world and one of Jane's main reasons for living. If Conrad *didn't* like them? What then?

Fiona's voice rang out once again. "You get axed from Team Truth, effective immediately. And before you go asking on what grounds, it's for being an incurable fool, young man. That's what it means."

Beau whistled under his breath, as if the situation were beyond his control. A man had to do what a man had to do. "You'll become our mortal enemy. A blood feud will ravage our futures from now until eternity."

His buddies nodded, showing their support.

Jane nodded, her mouth watering. "Axed. Mortal enemy. Blood." *Gimme my pancakes!*

"To help distract you from your hangryness, you should show them your board, Jane." Fiona peeked out from the door between kitchen and dining room. "Maybe it will also help you craft the perfect crime solving party to showcase your—"

"Why are you humoring her?" Conrad interjected.

"Because I recognize genius when I hear it, agent. Too bad for you if you can't say the same." Fiona humphed and disappeared again.

"How did you know about the—oh, never mind." Jane relinquished her silverware and popped to her feet. "Be right back."

She rolled the big white board from the office, where she'd stored it, to the kitchen, only nicking three walls. "Tell me if you need me to explain anything. Although it appears pretty self-explanatory to me." Different shades of yarn meant different things, the key in the right-hand corner. Simple. Easy.

Both Conrad and Beau grew wide-eyed and glazed as they surveyed her handiwork.

"The way your mind works." Conrad waved his fingers to indicate the photos, plethora of sticky notes, and all her many thought bubbles. "You have a thread for people who give you a bad vibe...and every single person is connected to it."

"That. What he said." Beau hiked his thumb at the agent without looking away from the dizzying, crisscrossing threads. Once again, his buddies nodded.

"Correct. And I stand by my assessment. But it's the photos that bother me most," she said, pointing from Robby to Blake to Jake. The images she'd printed from social media —some of the same snapshots she'd spotted in Ana's box of photos. "I mean, both guys claim someone impersonated them to clean out their savings. But who could pass themselves off as whom?" Wait. That was an excellent question. *Who could pass themselves off as whom?*

Jane positioned in front of the board and glanced from photo to photo. From certain angles, one or all of the guys could be mistaken as the other. There were big differences, of course, no two guys the same. Varying hair colors, skin tones, builds, shapes and vibes. And yet... yeah, there were similarities too. Big similarities. Especially among the photos of a guy kissing a girl's cheek. As if they all had come with the same default program.

What if one man had targeted the others? Thanks to Team Truth, she knew you only needed a driver's license and a bit of info memorized to drain an account. If the thief resembled the victim, the victim couldn't prove a crime occurred. No crime, no heat. Pure evil. As Blake could attest.

That's it! She knew it, felt it. That *must* be Ana's big story. The reason the journalist had gone on those dates with Robby—because there was *no* other excuse to date Robby, and that was an undeniable truth. And if the thief's identity was, in fact, Ana's big story, then it tied into speed dating, exactly as the journalist had believed.

So the thief, what? Attended speed dating events to find his next victim and have an excuse to ask personal questions?

Excitement bloomed. Forget Tiffany and Abigail and the desire for gold. A speed dater could have attended the Berdize events seeking to acquire the personal info of other daters. Then, after accessing their bank accounts, pinned the blame on the other daters. Yes! One of the sixteen *must be* involved in the killing, and Jane believed she had just narrowed it down to three, thanks to her (no doubt) scarily accurate bad vibes.

The Robber, aka Gravedigging Robby. Art Amour, aka too easy-going Jake. Sir Drinks A Lot, aka super petty Anthony, whom she'd let slip away from her radar for a bit. But no longer.

About to leave town Jake. Never stop throwing back Tony. On the hunt for gold Robby.

Yep. The more Jane played with their names, the more certain she was. They were her top three suspects. Solidified. Final answer. The evidence was stacking up. AKA her feelings said, *Ding, ding, ding.*

Whoever had killed Ana was a planner as much as a thief.

Tony, a lawyer who needed to stay organized to win cases. Robby, a gold hunter who'd known to learn Jane's schedule. Jake, a painter, used to paying close attention to the smallest details.

Snide Robby. Smiley Jake. Smug Tony. One of them had planted that thorn apple at the Garden to frame Jane, and he would pay.

New mission for the party: Focus totally on the trio. The widow and the ex-wife would get major side-eye, though.

"I know that look," Conrad said with a groan.

Beau groaned, too. "One or both of us is breaking a law in the next twenty-four hours, guaranteed."

"As if I'd let either one of you do my crime-ing. You're both too soft for the slammer. Unlike me. I've been there. Twice. I've seen things." Decided, Jane returned to the table and reclaimed her seat between Conrad and Beau. Just in time.

"Don't worry." Fiona placed multiple mountains of hotcakes on each side of the table. "There's more batter when we run out of these."

Rolex jumped down, hissed at Beau's friends, and sauntered off without biting or clawing. It was such a precious moment. Tears sprang to Jane's eyes.

"Eat, eat," Fiona commanded, placing a gravy bowl filled with warm syrup next to the hotcakes.

Team Truth and sidekicks dug in. Jane studied Conrad between shoveling bites of perfection, forking Beau any time he attempted to steal someone else's portion of the stack, laughing as Fiona regaled the group with the latest town gossip. Her special agent watched everyone at once, and he listened intently, giving nothing away. Well, not nothing. Twice he almost smiled or frowned; she wasn't sure which. But either way, her heart swelled. Not a single thing in the world beat this. Good food and better company. Or good company and better food.

Sometimes the living weren't so bad, after all.

"All right," Fiona said when the last crumb vanished. "I call this meeting of Team Truth to order. We've got a party to plan."

CHAPTER FIFTEEN

"Nothing wrong with a taste test!"
Whynot, North Carolina - Whynot Find Love Gathering
5 Matches Made!

*J*ane paced outside the door of a supply closet, her party mere minutes away from kick off. The Manor's kitchen provided a chaotic backdrop behind her, a chef and an array of wait staff puttering here and there, preparing trays of hors d'oeuvres.

With the help of the Berdize sisters and funds from Beau, Team Truth had booked and transformed the inn's event room into a veritable paradise of promised glitz and glamor. They used the Headliner for good this time—getting word out about the party. All last minute, all worth it. There'd been one itty bitty problem, however. Beau's outfit. He'd arrived in something similar to his attire for the speed dating event —shorts and flip flops and that just wouldn't do. Expecting such a travesty, Jane had prepared and grabbed an appropriate substitute before leaving the cottage.

"This is the last time I cave to your demands," he grumbled behind the door as he changed. "Next time, I'm putting my foot down. I mean it."

"And I promise I almost believe you," Jane responded, pausing and anchoring her hands on her hips. "Well? Let's see you."

"There was nothing wrong with my clothes." The knob turned, and Beau pushed the wood slab out of his way. "My T-shirt didn't make me want to crawl out of my skin."

Jane ran her gaze over the chocolate brown ensemble with wide, white stitching. The crushed velvet jacket was a bit too small, yet the ginormous pockets more than made up for it. The matching bell-bottom pants might be a... smidge too short. But with his collar popped, Beau's incredible style could not be denied. Much better.

"I was absolutely correct. Pops's clothing has character and looks amazing on you," she praised, giving him the classic *turn around and let me see the back* signal.

He glowered down at her. And he did not turn around.

Jane herself wore a shimmering gold taffeta creation with spaghetti straps, a scooped bodice and a short, flared skirt. A braided bun rested against her nape and showed off a small golden hat.

"How is this glitz and glamor?" he demanded, holding out his arms in a universal sign of exasperation.

"Um, how is it not? You're wearing the majesty of the seventies, bud. Think of yourself as an eccentric, jet-setting trendsetter." She moved to his side and patted his bulging bicep. "You're about to set the fashion world on fire, probably."

"If you say anything about the tight fit... " He gave a little growl and held both hands over his groin area.

She bit the corner of her lip to halt a laugh. Or to give him any clue that he might be, well, right. It was a very tight fit. "First of all, you're welcome. You'll earn more at auction now, guaranteed." She looped her arm through his and proceeded to the ballroom. "C'mon. Let's go catch ourselves a killer."

He complained as they proceeded down the hallway. She didn't catch full sentences, but she definitely detected words like "ridiculous" and "never again." He went quiet as soon as they reached the event room's entrance.

Jane surveyed the fruit of seventeen hours of frenzied hustle. An ivory and gold balloon arch led to a spacious ballroom with twinkle lights that dangled from the ceiling in cascading tiers. In back, a long table offered a feast of mini desserts, each seemingly dipped in molten gold. Smaller tables with huge floral centerpieces offered guests a place to mingle. To the left was a backdrop for selfies. To the right, an open bar, thanks to Beau and his mysterious fortune. And in the middle waited a dais with three podiums where Jane's "treasures" were displayed in clear, locked display cases guarded by Isaac, Holden, and Trick.

Beau's friends had provided the gold nuggets. Spray painted rocks? Fool's gold?

Fiona spotted Jane and rushed over, resplendent in a bold red gown. "There you are. Guests are lining up at the door, and they're getting restless. Shall we let them in?"

"As soon as Charlotte or Aubrey give us the go ahead." The pair stood off to the side, heads bent over a checklist.

Beau might be a fearsome military vet, a catcher and releaser of graverobbers, and an all-around good-guy baddie, but dread flared in his eyes. "Is it too late to cancel the auction?"

"Yes," Fiona and Jane replied in unison.

"According to the Headliner," Fiona continued, "everyone from recent college grads to grandmas are waiting for their shot at you, Beau. Go out there and prepare yourself to greet each person as they enter. Be sure to dazzle them just like we taught you and run up those bids." She pushed him toward the front doors.

As he stomped off, she grinned at Jane. "However you got Beau to agree to wear Gary's suit...I approve."

"If only Conrad was so easy to convince," Jane told her friend, and they shared a giggle.

Though her boyfriend had refused to show solidarity with Beau and don her Pops's *other* favorite leisure suit—a powder blue beauty—he'd worn a gold tie to match Jane's dress. Speaking of, where *was* Conrad, anyway? He'd been here a few minutes ago.

"All right, places everyone," called Charlotte Berdize, clapping her hands as servers hurried inside the room to take their posts. "I've been alerted by the front desk. The lobby is nearly over capacity, so we must get this show on the road."

Right. *Show time!* Tonight, Jane caught a killer. Or at least tried.

A door in back swung open, and Conrad strolled inside. As he closed the distance, he had eyes only for Jane. Jane, on the other hand, had eyes for the woman who wasn't far behind him. Agent Hightower, who wore a tight black dress perfect for her curves.

The moment the pair reached Jane's side, she hugged Conrad and whispered, "You invited her to my sting operation?"

Taking her hand, he said, "We're all on the same team."

Not exactly the denial she'd hoped. But, as his spice-scented warmth enveloped her, she forgave him for the horrendous crime.

Hightower nodded a greeting, her features devoid of emotion. "Hello, Jane." Her tone was devoid of emotion, too.

Some of Grandma Lily's advice rose to the surface of her mind. *Always be a lady—until you need to be a warrior.* Now was the time to be a lady. A gracious hostess. Jane forced a smile. "Hello. You look lovely today." Truth.

Now the agent blinked with surprise. "Thank you."

"If you'll excuse us," Conrad said to the agent and Fiona. With a hand on Jane's lower back, he led her toward the front doors, where Beau greeted guests as they poured inside the room.

Oh, look. There was Gus, the guy she'd met at Digging For Gold. Robby's friend. He'd brought a date. Not the same girl he'd left with after speed dating.

He spotted Jane and led the petite blonde on his arm in the other direction. Oops. Hmm. Maybe he ran from Conrad? It might be prudent to keep an eye on Mr. Gus tonight, along with the other three.

When Conrad steered her to the right, she frowned. "Where are we going?" A waiter passed by, and she almost grabbed a glass or two of peach julep. *Not tonight, Jay Bird.*

"We're walking around so I can keep you to myself before the chaos ensues."

She swallowed a groan. "Hardly. You want to give me some commands and warnings."

"No commands or warnings. I'm beginning to accept your adrenaline junkie ways. You'll have to accept the fact that I will always, without exception, do everything I can to protect you."

That was the second time he'd mentioned the adrenaline junkie thing. But he couldn't be more wrong. She preferred a quiet life...didn't she? "I won't ever complain about your protection. Allow me to offer a suggestion, however. In books and movies, the heroine's protector is usually shirtless. It's so their muscles scare the bad guys away. You should consider this kind of strategy."

He barked out a laugh. "Never change, sweetheart."

The rusty sound sparked a white-hot flush that traveled

over every inch of her skin. Better change the subject before she melted. "So. Did Hightower share anything more about what she'd learned during the interview with Robby?"

Not missing a beat, he replied, "Only that he blamed you for everything."

"He did what now?" Oh, the nerve of that man! Well, speak of the devil... Robby entered the ballroom with a girl Jane had never met, preceded by Abigail and Landon Kirkland, shovel guy.

First target acquired.

Both women wore puffy yellow ball gowns. Better to hide the gold they hoped to steal? Even as Jane bristled, she pasted a cheerful smile on her face. She'd *known* that bunch would take the bait.

Grinning, she steered Conrad their way to stop the group on their trek toward the podium to check out the gold.

The tall, slender, elegant brunette stuck her nose in the air. "Jane. Everyone else."

Abigail's version of a greeting.

"Nice to see you without ski masks," Jane said, sugar sweet. And, okay, yeah. A part of her might greatly anticipate the confrontation to come.

Landon blanched, rocking back on his heels.

Abigail raised her nose higher. "What are you even talking about?"

Robby bowed up, and the unfamiliar girl on his arm projected confusion. "I hear you were arrested—twice," he said with a sugar sweet tone of his own. His gaze darted to Conrad, then back to Jane, a layer of his confidence taking a hit. Nervous near the special agent? "Too bad I didn't get to see you in cuffs."

A tower of ice, Conrad stayed silent. But then, his glare said everything—and The Robber got the message.

"Yes. Well." Robby cleared his throat. "You've monopolized enough of our time." He led the group around her, moving deeper into the room.

"He is so guilty," Jane muttered.

Conrad remained silent, in full special agent mode, unwilling to confirm nor deny.

For the next hour, guests arrived and snacked and mingled, everyone dressed to the nines despite this being a last-minute party thrown by Cemetery Girl. She worried her two-time ex-lawyer Tony and Jake, new fiancé to the wealthy widow, had opted to bail, but they turned up within five minutes of each other. Tony had already imbibed, as evidenced by his red-rimmed, glassy eyes and slightly slurred words. Jake was all smiles at Tiffany's side.

Blake showed up solo, thanks to an "attendance" payment, courtesy of Beau. He appeared more hopeful than before. None of her suspects seemed to notice him, however.

Jane breathed in and exhaled, preparing for her part in the night's festivities. *This is happening!* "Phase two is soon to commence," she said, nearly giddy by the prospect. The launch of the one-man bachelor auction. This would lead to stage three—searching the vehicles of each suspect.

Someone had driven that thorn apple to her home. That someone might have trace amounts of soil in their trunk. Or an errant leaf. Maybe souvenirs that tied the driver to past crimes. Whatever! Perhaps that someone even kept fake IDs in his glove box or something. Worth a look, anyway, if nothing else.

"No throw downs tonight," Conrad said, squeezing her hand. "Please."

"I can't make promises."

Amid the throng, Jane took stock. Beau's friends remained on the podium with the gold, allowing no one to get too close. Beau himself shifted his weight from side to side, surrounded by women of all ages. Fiona bustled about, ensuring the top suspects never ran out of their chosen drinks, planning to steal their car keys as soon as an opportunity arose. Who would suspect a little oldish lady of theft?

Currently Blake sat at a table, observing.

Abigail and Robby remained close to the nuggets, whispering together, crafting an elaborate heist, no doubt.

Tony exchanged words with Hightower. Fishing for information about the case?

Gus danced with his date.

Jake never left Tiffany's side and, shocker of shockers, he never ceased smiling. How could the widow stand all that fawning? He even followed her to the bathroom, patiently waiting outside the door.

Jane and Conrad circled the room, moving from guest to guest. Witnessing the handsome lawman in his element was kind of amazing. He charmed everyone one-on-one while subtly steering the conversations, which allowed Jane to continue her observations of the couple.

They posed for a picture. Jake kissed Tiffany's cheek, as usual. Then she struck a new position. Again, he kept his face turned into hers. Another pose, another kiss on the cheek. Okay, that was suspicious, right? Almost as if he sought to avoid photographic evidence of his visage.

His vehicle gets searched first.

Excited, Jane kissed Conrad's cheek. "I'm gonna start the auction. Whatever happens, don't worry about me. I'll be fine. Promise. Okay, bye." She dashed off before he had a chance to respond. He didn't know about stage three, and she preferred to keep it that way.

Jane hunted down Charlotte, got the mic, and hurried to Beau's side. They climbed the dais side-by-side, his emerald eyes spitting fire at her.

His friend, Trick, said, "Nice suit, Sandman."

Sandman? His military nickname?

The other soldiers snickered.

"You or Fiona better be the one to purchase me, Jane," Beau softly growled.

"And deprive you of a possibly real romantic connection? No, we aren't that cruel. Plus, Eunice probably plans to be here tonight." But she had spotted no sign of the beautiful accountant she knew would be perfect for him. "Bonus. The money you make for this date will allow me to reimburse you for this entire shindig."

The overhead lights dimmed as soon as they reached the center. Next, a spotlight glowed over them. Conversations died, all attention focused fully on the stage.

Facing the darkened crowd, she lifted the mic. "Good evening, everyone. Allow me to welcome you to this celebration of my amazing luck of striking it mega rich, and true love. Please give a round of applause to my co-hosts, the Berdize sisters. If anyone makes a match tonight, all credit goes to them." A condition of their aid.

Once the clapping died down, Jane motioned to the smoke show at her side. "Many of you probably recognize Beau Harden. A hometown hero eager to make some sweet lady's dreams come true."

"Jane," Beau hissed with his teeth clenched.

She smiled brightly, ignoring him. "Beau has graciously agreed to plan—and attend!—a romantic evening with the highest bidder. There are only two requirements. You must be single and breathing. I kid, I kid. You only need to be single."

Chuckles resounded throughout the room.

Since she'd promised to also make this a congratulatory bash honoring Tiffany's upcoming nuptials, Jane added, "But before I receive the first bid, I'd like to take a moment to honor our own Tiffany Hotchkins for her recent engagement. Let's raise a glass to Tiffany and Jake."

While not exactly enthusiastic, most of the crowd played along. "To Tiffany and Jake."

The spotlight, operated by Charlotte, swung to Tiffany, who preened and waved. Jake's smile wasn't quite as bright. Jane caught sight of Tony, Robby and Gus, too. They huddled around each other like co-conspirators.

What if they'd all worked together?

Eager to begin the car search, Jane motioned for Charlotte to flood the crowd with more light, then she gestured for Aubrey Berdize to take the stage and handed over the mic. One of the sibling's workers rushed up to place a tripod on the stage. A sheet covered whatever topped it.

"Hey, guys," Aubrey called amid cheers. "I gotta give a big, warm welcome to the patrons of Digging for Gold. This event is for you. Our way of saying thank you."

Louder cheers rang out, some exuberant, some half-hearted.

"I know our ladies are ravenous for a go at Beau Harden, but I'd like to unveil our plans for The Tatiana Irons Memorial Garden on Main Street." She tugged off the sheet, revealing a landscape design for a beautiful round planter, complete with river rock, decorative lighting, and delicate ironworks. A picture of a smiling Ana was clipped to the side of the poster. "The monument will be nestled in the northeast corner of the River Bottom Park."

The crowd dutifully oohed and ahhed.

With the added light, Jane was able to scan the sea of faces as Aubrey pointed out elements of the garden. Tony had returned to the bar. Hmm. Abigail remained zeroed in on the "gold" nuggets. Jake whispered something to Tiffany, who grinned. Robby stared at the board—or Ana's photo—with a mix of sadness and anger molding his features.

Either one of them was without a heart, or none of them

were guilty. Could Jane have gotten this wrong from the beginning?

"All right. Let's give another round of applause to Jane Ladling for agreeing to display her treasure," Aubrey said, Jane's cue to leave the stage and make a beeline for Fiona, who waited by the kitchen door as planned. "Now. Who's ready to buy themselves a slice of man meat and win one of those nuggets as their very own?"

The throng erupted with genuine excitement.

Fiona greeted her with a smile, and together they hurried through the kitchen door while the masses were distracted. They passed a service station wild with activity as wait staff refilled their trays.

"Did you snag all the keys?" Jane asked.

"Two out of three. Robby was too guarded. Like a feral cat in a room full of rocking chairs."

Well. Robby was probably the killer, then. "We'll enter his car, one way or another."

"You bet we will." Fiona held up a small, black velvet pouch. "Brought my lock picking tools. Never leave home without it."

Jane gaped at her. "You keep lock picking tools?"

"Doesn't everyone?"

Nope. But she would from now on. "You know how to use them?"

A snort. "Hon. How else do you think I found out my second husband had an affair? His desk drawers didn't stand a chance."

Well. "I'll take Jake's sports car. You get into Tony's sedan, and we'll meet at Robby's. If we don't find anything, we'll break into Gus's vehicle too."

Fiona nodded her agreement. "Sounds like a plan."

Jane paused. "Be sure to take out your phone and video

everything. We need to be able to prove we found what we find."

Firm resolve entered the other woman's dark eyes. "Good thinking. If it implicates us in a crime ourselves and we end up in prison again, so be it. Justice will be served!"

Agreed. "Go Team Truth!"

They exited the building and entered the maxed out parking lot, breaking apart to begin the search.

CHAPTER SIXTEEN

"Be FAB—Finally a Bride!"
Bridal Veil, Oregon - Kiss the Miss Goodbye
100% Matched!

*J*ane discovered Jake's sleek little sports car in a prime spot marked "Reserved," perfectly illuminated by an historic streetlamp. Great. Wonderful. But was the vehicle made at NASA? Not a single knob or handle in sight. Only touchscreens and digital displays, with a useless key. None of the buttons worked.

She had to stop her video recording long enough to watch a tutorial on her cell, but she finally managed to press the correct sequence on the keypad and force a door to open.

A quick look over her shoulder. No sign of anyone, not even Fiona, who had hopefully found Tony's sedan.

Using her phone as a flashlight, Jane examined the driver's side interior, the passenger's side, and the back seat. Black leather interior. All the latest bells and whistles. Not a speck of dirt or a single piece of trash. No stolen IDs in the glove box or center console. Clean. Almost too clean.

Disappointed but determined, she watched another video to learn how to pop the trunk...yes! Success. After starting another video recording, she rushed to the back of the vehicle only to draw up short with a gasp. Jake! He stood statue still with his hands resting in his pockets, staring at her. For the first time, he wasn't smiling. Or with Tiffany. Jake and Jane were alone.

She stuffed her phone in the only pocket of her dress, lest he attempt to snatch the device from her hand. Though the camera no longer showed Jake, it continued recording, ready to capture the ensuing conversation. Considering she stood next to the evidence of her crime—the open trunk—that might not be such a great thing for her.

"Um. Hi," she began.

"Hello, Jane." His tone was pleasant, but his face remained an emotionless mask. However, the stiffness of his shoulders conveyed only the slightest hint of tension.

Ignoring the rapid beat of her heart, she pretended to be casual, too. "Okay, so, you caught me. Surprise! We plan to decorate your car. Obviously." Not a lie. She was planning to do it...now. As long as he was innocent, of course. "I'm sure you know the drill. Shoe polish on the windows, cans and old shoes dragging from the bumper. The wedding works! I mean, we gotta do everything tonight since you and Tiff are heading out on your trip tomorrow." Jane raised the volume of her voice, hoping to reach Fiona. "My helper should arrive any minute."

His gaze lowered to her hands—her empty hands. Not a bottle of shoe polish in sight.

"Is your helper the old lady?" He propped his hip against the car, cool and laid-back, then cupped a hand around one side of his mouth and called, "Shout if you hear us, Fiona. Someone? Anyone?"

Her knees wobbled, her fingers curling to create fists. A

cruel glint had entered his eyes, obliterating his air of inno-cence; the man in front of her was absolutely guilty of some-thing. "Did you hurt my friend?" she demanded.

"There was no need. I'm not a cruel guy, Jane. Contrary to what you might think, murder is never my preference. Did I push her into Miller's trunk and lock her inside? Yes. But she's fine. And don't expect your boyfriends to rush to your rescue. I blocked the inn's exits and I'll be long gone before anyone is able to get free. But first, I'm curious. What gave me away?"

"You'll have to be more specific," she grated. Was he telling the truth about Fiona?

"You'd like a confession? Very well. I killed Ana Irons. I planted jimsonweed at your cemetery, hacked into your security feed to erase my presence if necessary, and waited for the day Ana scheduled a visit with you. When the day ultimately dawned, I dressed as Robby Waynes and poisoned her coffee. Now. What gave me away?"

Her jaw dropped. Uh…. Had he just confessed to premed-itated murder? And computer hacking! And Jane had recorded it? She replayed his words inside her head. *I killed Ana Irons.*

He had.

Knew he was guilty of something! She might be the world's greatest amateur-bordering-on-professional sleuth. He was the one. The thief and the killer. Art Amour *and* the Robber. Which was kind of disappointing, honestly. She'd really hoped to be the one to put Robby in prison. But just how many other nicknames pointed to Jake? With his multiple identities, the possibilities could be endless.

"Jane," he prompted. "Stalling will not help you."

"Give me a moment to put my thoughts together. You attended the speed dating events to pick your victims. You impersonated other men and took their money. You cleaned out Blake and Robby's accounts, then pitted them against each other. You preyed upon poor Tiffany, hoping to drain her dry too. Ana learned about your heinous crimes, and you killed her, getting her out of the way, framing me. And if not me, Robby. You called Tiffany while she was at the salon to, what? Build an alibi? Perform your dirty deeds dressed up as Robby, while calling her as Jake and claiming she hung up on you."

"Exactly right," he told her, sounding bored. "Ana complained about your many harassing phone calls. It led her to work on a story about you and the cemetery's gold. She planned to speak with you the morning she died. And I hoped to buy the cemetery once you were out of the way. With Tiffany's money, of course."

"Of course." Jane reeled, almost dizzy with success. She'd had just scored an all-out confession. How many others could say the same? "Look at you." She shook her head at him. "You're not even sorry, are you?"

He smiled a little, but it was a cold facsimile of the one he'd always projected at Tiffany. His victims never saw him coming, did they? "I'm quite wealthy. What do I have to be sorry about? Other than your lack of an answer to my question." He rocked back on his heels, rattling whatever he held in his pocket. A switchblade? A gun? Did he plan to kill Jane too? "I'm a very careful man. I like to learn from my mistakes."

Stall him. Keep him talking. He might believe he'd taken Fiona, Conrad and Beau out of the equation, but he didn't know the members of Team Truth like she did. Actually, he didn't know Jane, either.

"Are you going to kill me as soon as I finish explaining?" she asked and gulped.

"I told you. There's no need. I have what I wanted from Tiffany, as well as your gold. Your three guard dogs never noticed when I made an exchange." He grinned again, a sharp baring of his teeth, completely unaware he'd replaced fakes with fakes. "I'll disappear seconds after we finish this conversation, never to be heard from or seen by the people of this town again."

Leave? No! She took a step forward, instinct demanding she grab him. But she caught herself before contact. Conrad had given her a self-defense lesson during the previous case, and she utilized those skills now. First up, assessing the target. Did Jake have a weapon or not? "The last thing I'm gonna do is help you deceive your next victim."

"Ana was...necessary. Too nosy for her own good." He pulled his hands from his pockets. Yep. A folded knife waited in his grip. "I won't ask again, Jane. What gave me away?"

Her breath hitched when she spotted Fiona several yards back, sneaking through the darkness with a tire iron clutched in her hand. To keep him focused on Jane, she babbled her reasons in a rush. "Well, for starters, you only recently moved to town. That was a dead giveaway. In my experience as a killer catcher, it's the new guy one hundred percent of the time. And you were too nice. Always smiling and being kind. It was off-putting. Plus, art is supposed to speak to people. Yours screams, *I'm trying too hard to be like the greats*. Also, I noticed right away that your name rhymes with Blake's. Lastly, you treated Tiffany like a queen. It was super suspicious."

He narrowed his eyes. "You don't want to be honest. That's fine. I'm afraid we've run out of time." He took a step toward her, only to tense and spin, sensing Fiona, who was almost upon him.

Jane didn't think about her next actions. She kicked Jake in the back of the knee. As he dropped to the concrete, Fiona swung the tire iron with the grace of a swan, nailing him in the shoulder. A pained grunt exploded from him as he toppled. The switchblade went flying across the distance.

"Who are you calling old?" Fiona hit him again when he tried to stand. "Sixty-two is young."

He growled and huffed and labored to his hands and knees, as if to strike.

"Don't hurt my young friend!" Jane threw herself at him, shoving him to his face. His chin crashed against the concrete first, and he roared, spitting blood.

"That's for framing Jane!" Fiona swung the tire iron again and again, smacking his butt while Jane draped herself over his back. "And that's for killing poor Ana."

"And ruining my garden!"

"Jane!" Conrad's voice drifted over the darkness. "She's over here!"

Footsteps sounded. Suddenly he was there, pulling her off Jake and checking her over. Hightower came in behind him to help the now admitted thief to his feet. Beau was right behind her; he rushed over to hug Fiona and look her over.

"I'm fine, I'm fine," Jane told Conrad between panting breaths. "But he did it. Jake Stephenson is the killer." She pointed to the awful man. "He confessed everything. He's a conman and a murderer and a framer, and he stole my gold. He came at me with a knife, but it skidded somewhere."

"You don't have any gold, Jane. And we will find the knife." Conrad cupped her face and forced her gaze to meet his. "I am so mad at you right now. Do not take any more years off my life. Sit in that little plot of grass over there, under that beam of light, and stay there until I collect you. You and Fiona both."

"Okay, okay. But for the record, I just solved my second murder. And my plan worked. Throw a party and boom! Case closed. Put *that* in your Jane Ladling handbook."

He made a choking sound before giving her a scorching

look she felt all the way down to her toes. Then he inserted himself in the action as Jane and Fiona obeyed, settling on the plot of grass. It wasn't long before Beau joined them.

"Don't leave us in suspense," Fiona said to him. "Who bought you?"

"Abigail Waynes-Kirkland," he grated.

What! Abigail got to go on a date with Beau? "No. Absolutely not. I forbid it."

Still grating, he told them, "She agreed to pay a thousand dollars."

"Well." Jane pursed her lips. "I suppose you can survive a *few* hours with her. But you are *not* to enjoy a single second."

"Arrest those two women," Jake shouted at Hightower, ending the auction conversation at the perfect spot. "I noticed my keys were missing. I came out to make sure I hadn't locked them inside and I found that woman—" he pointed to Jane— "stealing my car. The next thing I knew, they were beating me with a tire iron!"

Tiffany rushed up, her heels clacking on the asphalt. "What's going on? What's happening?" She threw herself against Jake, clinging to him before brushing the dirt from his shirt and smoothing his hair. "Oh, babe. Is Jane trying to blame us for Ana's death?"

So. Tiffany *had* attempted to investigate Jane at dinner. Only the widow had done it to save her man.

Jane geared up to shout a rebuke, but Hightower beat her to it, saying, "Calm down, Mr. Stephenson. We'll get this sorted out."

"Actually, I've already sorted it," Conrad said, a tower of strength. "As of this morning, the Manor has acquired the services of Peach State Security. As an independent contractor working with the agency, I helped Beau Harden install security cameras throughout the parking lot. They provide live feed of video and audio, both of which are being monitored through my cell phone. I have a recording of Mr. Stephenson's confession. I can assure you, Jake Stephenson killed Tatiana Irons. He robbed Robby Waynes and Blake Crawford as well."

Ohhhh. Sneaky, sneaky Conrad. Wracked by shivers, Jane wrapped her arms around her middle. That was almost as delicious as a peach julep.

"No. No, that can't be true." Tiffany reared back, her features twisting with horror. "Jake?"

"I have a recording too, and I can verify this." She whipped out her cell phone, started the video and played what she'd recorded.

Her own voice seeped from the speaker. *"Give me a moment to put my thoughts together. You attended the speed dating events to pick your victims. You impersonated other men and took their money. You cleaned out Blake and Robby's accounts, then pitted them against each other. You preyed upon poor Tiffany, hoping to drain her dry too. Ana learned about your heinous crimes, and you killed her, getting her out of the way, framing me. And if not me, Robby. You called Tiffany while she was at the salon to, what? Build an alibi? Perform your dirty deeds dressed up as Robby, while calling her as Jake and claiming she hung up on you."*

Jake's emotionless voice announced, *"Exactly right. Ana complained about your many harassing phone calls. It led her to work on a story about you and the cemetery's gold. She planned to speak with you the morning she died. And I hoped to buy the cemetery once you were out of the way. With Tiffany's money, of course."*

Tiffany gasped, the color draining from her cheeks. "You wanted the gold. Jane's and mine. So many little things make sense now. You heard my husband found gold at the cemetery and you hoped to steal from me. You *used* me." With a sob, the widow grabbed the forgotten tire iron and swung it in Jake's direction. He bolted, and Hightower gave chase, quickly tackling him to the ground.

Conrad urged the still-sobbing widow to sit before she passed out. Which she did–sit down, not pass out.

And like that, it was over, everything under control. Hightower loaded a cuffed Jake into the back of her car, careful of his head. Conrad spoke with Tiffany until Abigail arrived to hug her, glare at Jane, then escort her friend into a vehicle.

Sheriff Moore arrived, flashing red and blue lights over the scene. Jane popped to her feet, and Beau helped Fiona to hers. The sheriff exited his vehicle, strolled over, and doffed his hat at them.

"Fine work this evening," he said.

Jane beamed at him. "Thank you."

He briefly glanced in her direction, his focus returning to Fiona. "If you hadn't kept your wits about you, Fee, and surprised him with that tire iron, tonight might have had a very different ending."

"You heard about that, did you?" Fiona fluffed her hair.

"I did. Conrad has kept me apprised of the situation."

From there, things happened quickly. New agents arrived and took everyone's statement and then released them. The Berdize sisters cleaned up the party, thrilled that people would talk about it for weeks to come. Months even. Jane marveled through it all. Team Truth had done it. They'd worked together, kind of, and solved a case, fully exonerating her good name. And they'd had fun, each of them. Because of their efforts, justice would be served.

∼

As the moon set the Garden aglow with silvery light, Jane keyed into the cottage. Conrad, Beau, his three friends, and

Fiona were quick on her heels. Too bad Hightower and the sheriff couldn't join them. Hightower had to get Jake situated and finish some paperwork; Sheriff Moore planned to "sleep like the dead" now that a killer was off the streets. If Eunice Park had bothered to show up to the event, she could have come to the cottage too.

Naturally, everyone gravitated to the kitchen. "Who's hungry?" Jane asked.

Multiple shouts of "Me!" rang out.

"Why don't I make my blueberry pancakes?" Fiona offered, not looking the least bit tired. "We did good tonight. We all deserve a reward."

"Yes!" Jane blurted. "We accept. All of us. We insist you start cooking immediately!"

"Immediately," Conrad and Beau called as one, as if they had rehearsed it.

"I knew you loved the pancakes." As the men took their seats around the table, she stood with Fiona at the head of the room, smiling at Conrad. "Because who in their right mind wouldn't?"

He smiled back, making her heart leap. "Sweetheart." Uh-oh. The tone. The one that meant he was gearing up to throw down a lecture. "It's not the pancakes."

Beau coughed, and that cough sounded an awful lot like the word "Don't."

Don't what, exactly? "What do you mean, it's not the pancakes? Let's be clear. Life isn't worth living without the pancakes, Conrad."

Whiskey eyes twinkling, he wiped his mouth, as if to wipe the growing smile away. But he failed. "It's the pancakes. One hundred percent."

Okay. All right. For some reason, a wild thought struck her just then. What if she became a private investigator? A *paid* one. The cemetery could use an influx of cash. The trust and her meager stipend didn't allow for many updates.

It was worth considering, anyway. Granted, she had no true experience or schooling and her talents questionable, if not non-existent, but you couldn't argue with success. Fingers crossed someone else died soon, and she got to prove herself a third time. Once could have been an accident, twice an anomaly. But a third time, well, that would put the nail in the coffin. In a good way.

Not that she wanted anyone new to die. Whatever. It had been a long night.

"Did someone mention pancakes?" Isaac prompted.

Right. "Why don't I help you with the baking, Fiona." Maybe they had leftover supplies for a glass or eight of peach julep.

As she and Fiona busied themselves in the kitchen, Jane's heart grew light. Later, as they sat at the table with the guys, scarfing down blueberry pancakes and peach julep as if the world were ending in the morning, laughing, and teasing and glad to be alive, her spirit felt lighter.

When the last crumb had been consumed, she glanced in Conrad's direction. His heavy stare sent a glorious cascade of shivers down her spine.

"Just think, Conrad," Fiona said, patting Jane's hand. "If you had listened to Jane's theory about the rhyming names, you could have solved this case right at the start."

"Is madness contagious?" He looked between them. "I'm asking for myself."

Beau and company snorted and snickered.

"I'm sure I don't know what you mean." Fiona faked a yawn and stretched her arms over her head. "Time for this gal to go home and grab her beauty Zs."

The group broke up after that. Jane hugged everyone

goodbye. Beau received an added earlobe tweak and Fiona got a kiss on the cheek.

Conrad lingered behind her—because she caught his hand when he headed for the door. He got the message and stayed put, and she was glad. She wasn't ready for him to leave. When the last vehicle eased from the drive, Jane shut the door and faced him, sealing them together.

She turned and met his heated gaze, her pulse jumping, erratic. The scent of cedar and spice fogged her head. She couldn't think—but then, she didn't want to think. A lot had happened tonight. More than solving a case and catching a killer. Jake had carried a knife. At any time, he could have ended her life. But here she was. Alive and well. With a boyfriend she liked very much.

Someone patient and kind. Understanding. Willing to wait for her and get her out of prison whenever necessary. Someone who found her charming instead of weird. Who took care of her fur-child. Why not let him in, at least a little? Why not take a chance on him?

Why put her trust in a curse rather than the flesh and blood male who'd proven himself time and time again?

Licking her lips, she pressed her back against the wood slab and rasped, "Are you going to kiss me now?"

He flattened his palms beside her temples, one at a time, his gaze never dropping hers. "Do you want me to?" he asked.

"I... do." More than anything.

His pupils flared over his irises. "Then yes. I'm going to kiss you now."

And he did.

~

Up Next:
Game of Graves
Book 3 in the Jane Ladling Mystery Series

～

This book is dedicated to all the readers who took to Jane, Fiona, Rolex and prefer Conrad to Beau. With special thanks to Leni Kauffman and forever love to Naomi Lane.

-Gena Showalter

This book is dedicated to all the readers who took to Jane, Fiona, Rolex and prefer Beau to Conrad. With special thanks to Leni Kauffman and forever love to Naomi Lane.

-Jill Monroe

～

NON-FICTION:
   All Write Already
   All Write Already Workbook
   The Write Life
   Write Now! An All Write Already Journal

JANE LADLING COZY MYSTERY SERIES:
   Romancing the Gravestone
   No Gravestone Left Unturned
   Game of Graves

ABOUT GENA SHOWALTER

Gena Showalter is the New York Times and USA TODAY bestselling author of multiple "unputdownable" series in paranormal, contemporary, and young adult romance.

Learn more about Gena, her menagerie of rescue dogs, and all her upcoming books at genashowalter.com

ALSO BY GENA SHOWALTER

Immortal Enemies

Start with: Heartless

·

Rise of the Warlords

Start with: The Warlord

·

Lords of the Underworld

Start with: The Darkest Night

·

White Rabbit Chronicles

Start with: Alice in Zombieland

·

Tales of an Extraordinary Girl

Start with: Playing with Fire

·

Everlife

Start with: Firstlife

·

Original Heartbreakers

Start with: The Secret Fling

·

Angels of the Dark:

Start with: Wicked Nights

·

Otherworld Assassins

Start with: Last Kiss Goodnight

.

Gena's Complete List of Releases:

GenaShowalter.com/books

ABOUT JILL MONROE

Jill Monroe is the international best selling author of over fifteen novels and novellas. Her books are available across the globe and *The Wrong Bed: Naked Pursuit* has been adapted for the small screen for Lifetime Movie Network.

When not writing, Jill makes her home in Oklahoma with her husband, enjoys daily walks with her dog Zoey, texting with her two daughters who are away at college and collecting fabric for items she'll sew poorly.

Learn more about Jill at jillmonroe.com

ALSO BY JILL MONROE

Sworn Series:

Sworn Promises

Sworn Duty

Sworn By A Kiss

Sworn Protector

.

Wrong Bed Series

Naked Thrill

Naked Pursuit*

*(Now a movie from Lifetime Movie Network)

.

From Hallmark:

At The Heart of Christmas

.

Spicy Romance:

Fun & Games

Treasure in the Sand (novella)

.

Jill's Complete List of Releases:

jillmonroe.com/allbooks

Made in the USA
Las Vegas, NV
27 December 2023